KRONOS

'Guy Adams is either barking mad or a genius, I haven't decided.' Mark Chadbourn

The author of the novels *The World House* and its sequel *Restoration*, Guy Adams gave up acting five years ago to become a full-time writer. This was silly, but thankfully he's kept busy, writing bestselling humour titles based on TV show *Life on Mars* or *Torchwood* novels *The House That Jack Built* and *The Men Who Sold The World*.

He has also written a pair of original Sherlock Holmes novels, *The Breath of God* and *The Army of Doctor Moreau* as well as a biography of actor Leonard Rossiter and an updated version of Neil Gaiman's *Don't Panic: Douglas Adams & The Hitch-Hiker's Guide to the Galaxy*.

His website is: www.guyadamsauthor.com

GUY ADAMS

KRONOS

Published by Arrow Books in association with Hammer 2011

2 4 6 8 10 9 7 5 3 1

Copyright © Guy Adams 2011

Kronos is based on the classic Hammer film, *Captain Kronos Vampire Hunter*,
written and directed by Brian Clemens and released in 1974

First published in Great Britain in 2011 by
Arrow Books in association with Hammer
Random House, 20 Vauxhall Bridge Road,
London SW1V 2SA

www.randomhouse.co.uk
www.hammerfilms.com

Addresses for companies within The Random House Group Limited can be
found at: www.randomhouse.co.uk/offices.htm

The Random House Group Limited Reg. No. 954009

A CIP catalogue record for this book
is available from the British Library

ISBN 9780099556244

The Random House Group Limited supports The Forest Stewardship
Council (FSC®), the leading international forest certification organisation.
Our books carrying the FSC label are printed on FSC® certified paper.
FSC is the only forest certification scheme endorsed by the leading
environmental organisations, including Greenpeace. Our paper
procurement policy can be found at:
www.randomhouse.co.uk/environment

Typeset by SX Composing DTP, Rayleigh, Essex
Printed and bound by CPI Group (UK) Ltd, Croydon, CR0 4YY

KRONOS

Foreword by Brian Clemens

Back in the 1970s I had just finished writing and producing *Dr Jekyll & Sister Hyde* for Hammer, who then asked me to write and direct a vampire movie. Not a great fan of the genre, I immediately ran several of their previous films on the subject and came to the conclusion that the villain was the most compelling character, there was a lack of humour and, worst of all, they all seemed to have the same storyline – always ending up with poor Christopher Lee being staked through the heart. It really needed some fresh air and hence I created Kronos, which is Greek for 'time', because anticipating a series of movies, I left myself free to move through different time eras if necessary. I also created a whole new vampire lore, again giving myself room to vary the format and introduce some variety – plus humour here and there.

Kronos was a kind of Marvel comics hero, with some touches that made him hip in younger eyes. I had some grandiose ideas that budget prevented me using, such as I wanted Kronos to travel in a golden coffin – on the basis that to fight your enemy you have to think, feel and know him.

The movie was barely promoted but, I am happy to say, has since become a cult, and a recent celebration screening in London saw a full house and others queuing around the block to obtain autographs ... and now, at last, in the capable hands of Guy Adams, Kronos is back! The novel is exciting, remains true to the original concept and, who knows, may herald another movie? I hope so.

I guess that if enough of you fans (and your friends) buy enough copies of this book, you will have done your bit to make it happen. Thanks.

August 2011

One

Petra Is Dying

I'm dying. It may not look like it as I sit here amongst the late cover of campion flowers, but I am dying. We all are.

Dearest Ann is combing my hair and the sunshine throws flashes in the small mirror that I'm holding. I can see my face in the mirror. It is a good face, a beautiful face. That sounds horribly conceited but it would be pointless to lie. I'm lucky: I was born with a face that makes others do what I want. That's the greatest gift God can give.

Despite its beauty, the face is what makes me realise I'm dying. Looking at it, I can remember when it was smaller, chubbier, covered in freckles. I hated those freckles. It seems no time at all since Ann and I were running through these woods. Chasing, laughing, climbing trees. Now we sit and obsess on each other's beauty and the only thing we chase are boys (and they're only too happy to be caught). When did those freckles vanish? When did I? Our lives are like summers, that's what I think – they burn hot and become winter before you know it. I'm dying. We all are.

Ann runs off into the trees to find flowers for my hair.

I watch her go. Sweet Ann: if only she knew she was just as pretty as me. She is always the quiet one, the one who hangs back a few steps, the one who thinks she could never quite stand shoulder to shoulder with me. Would I want it any other way? Oh God, I hope so – am I that vain?

A light breeze passes through the trees, the ghost of winter come to visit. It won't be a ghost much longer. Just a few short weeks and the cold will come, the flowers will die, the leaves will fall and the mornings will start in darkness. We'll be breaking the ice on the water troughs so that the cows can drink.

I lean back against the tree, feeling the rough bark pressing red brands into my skin. The sunlight falls in thin shards, like a broken mirror, through the branches around me. I feel dreamy. I press back against the bark harder still, wanting to keep focused on the here and now as my mind threatens to wander away on the new-found chill in the air.

There are footsteps behind me, a crunch of leaves and a crack of twigs. I decide that I will tell Ann how beauti - ful she is, maybe even curl the flowers she has picked into her own hair rather than mine. I turn and smile at her but it's not Ann, it's someone just as beautiful, someone with a face that makes me do what it wants.

I lift my head and the hair that Ann has so carefully brushed catches in the wind and makes a grab for freedom even as that beautiful mouth descends on mine. I sink into a dream of dead summers from which I'll never wake.

Two

Dr Marcus Feels the Devil

I always dream of ambushes. Even here, in the warm and beautiful forest that I have loved these last few years, I imagine every ditch and shadow to be filled with the enemy. Their swords are drawn, they're waiting to pounce. The next moment, the very next one, will bring blood and fear. Such is the effect of war on a man.

The fighting has been over – for me at least – for nearly eight years. Now I am a country doctor. My patients suffer from aches and vapours, not musket-shot and knife wounds. Ireland is distanced by more than the sea: it is a country and a battlefield lost to time. And yet, still, I can remember the sound of cannon fire, the smell of gunpowder and blood. I find myself tensed, teeth grinding, eyes closed, waiting for the killing blow when no such blow can possibly fall. I suspect that the effects of war are nigh on incurable.

There are no foreign soldiers lurking in wait as I encourage my horse around a bend in the track. Nobody drops down from the branches above, a knife in their teeth. The slight creaking I can hear is the wind pressing the wood of the trees, not the strain of leather gauntlets as fingers pull back a bowstring.

I will survive this journey.

I know this.

God, how I wish I knew this.

'Ann?' The girl is standing in the middle of the track, staring into the trees as if she has fallen asleep on her feet. I recognise her, of course – a doctor knows every - body, he brings them into the world and sends them back out again. 'Ann, are you all right?'

She gives no sign of having heard me, just stands there, eyes unblinking.

I tie up the horse – poor reluctant Jenny, getting old enough now for every journey to be a chore rather than a pleasure – and walk over to Ann. She gives no sign of being aware of my presence. I could be no more solid than the breeze (which seems to have grown stronger since I dismounted, pulling dead leaves in cords around my ankles as if hoping to trip me up).

All of a sudden I become convinced that the war has shown me nothing. That the very worst that can be witnessed in this world is about to show itself here and now. I have no idea where this sudden conviction comes from: is it something glimpsed in Ann's eyes? Is it yet another hangover from the war? Wherever it hails from, it's all-consuming. Something terrible is coming. It will make pretty daisies of the red, battlefield flowers of an Irish field, those thick splayed petals that blossom from a man's ribcage when the cannon has found its mark. It will turn that smell of singed meat and burned straw that hung over the torched villages into the clean

4

freshness of a Christmas wind. There is something here, something so awful that I will die to see it. I have no idea where this certainty comes from but, once gripped, I cannot imagine being free. I have survived this long but no more. Death, laughing, has finally found me on the quiet tracks of this fair woodland.

'Ann?' I ask once more, the sound of my voice almost terrifying enough to force a scream from me. 'Ann, what is it?'

I look over my shoulder, following her gaze, and understand what it is that has struck her insensible.

Dear God, what have we done to bring such madness here?

Three

A Footman's Final Thoughts

'My name,' says the small hunchback as he leans over me, 'is Professor Herbert Grost. This may seem small recompense given your current situation' – and he's right, my life is bleeding hot onto the stone steps beneath me and I find I don't altogether care – 'but we do try not to kill the innocent.'

'Urggh,' I reply, which is as much as can be expected of me in the circumstances.

Loud noises begin to echo from the entrance hall and out onto the front step.

Grost loads a flintlock pistol and turns towards the open doorway. He fires the gun and then returns his attention to me while he reloads. 'But sometimes you just have to think of the greater good,' he says. 'I mean, jobs aren't easy to come by, I know that, but if you're working for the forces of evil you've made a choice, haven't you? Every man needs to eat but does he think first of his soul or of his belly?'

I'd known the answer to that once. Of course I had. Given how things have worked out for me I might have been wrong, of course.

Grost turns and fires the pistol again. He shouts into the hall: 'No, please don't thank me – he was only about to put that axe in your pretty blond head, after all.'

There is a reply but I can't hear it. Something flies past my line of vision, something small, round and dripping. It takes me a second to recognise it as the head of Gerry Kaveney, one of the stablehands. I'd been drinking with Gerry only three nights ago, talking about the usual stuff: how many new students had enrolled, how long they would last . . .

'Take the current situation,' continues Grost. 'I don't care how many mouths you have to feed, using a finishing school to fill the bed of a succubus is hard to justify. What had these poor girls done to deserve such an ignoble death? Poor innocents . . .'

You'd be surprised, I think. They'd been heartless bitches, most of them. Never a polite word or a kind smile for a working man.

'So,' Grost continues, moving out of my eyeline for a moment as he walks back to the coach they'd arrived in. Nice-looking vehicle, I'd thought, expecting yet another pampered student-to-be rather than a sword blade in my belly. 'When we heard about this place from one of the poor grieving parents, well, we could hardly stand by and let things continue. Once it became clear that the entire teaching staff were revenants under the control of the elusive Madame Loubrette . . .' Grost returns, carrying a small wooden crate, 'Oh . . . it was us that took your geography teacher, by the way – in order to gather information, you understand.' He looks ruminative. 'He would have appreciated the irony in his eventual death,

I imagine,' he says. 'He was certainly spread far and wide.'

The noises from inside have been receding for a while as the other man – the one who looked like a Prussian, the one with the bloody sword – moves deeper inside the building.

'Anyway,' Grost says, shifting the case in his hands so that it's easier to carry, 'having discovered how easy it would be to deal with the lot of you we thought we'd better just get on with it. The Captain's a busy man – places to ransack, creatures to stake, I'm sure you can imagine.' Grost tuts and then shakes his head. 'And to think that Cromwell fought for a 'pure' and holy England. Things are worse now then ever. There's nothing the devil feeds off better than a puritanical heart . . . enforced abstinence makes for a sinful world.' He looks down at me and, quite absurdly, smiles. 'Politics, eh? See you in a moment,' he says. 'If you're still alive, that is.'

Grost disappears inside the house and for a couple of minutes I listen to the sounds and try to imagine what's happening. Then my mind begins to wander and I think about home, about the small fishing village where I grew up. I can see the billowing sails and smell the tang of the lobster pots. I can't help but wonder at what point my life took such a downward turn. How had that young boy, gazing up at the masts and dreaming of the boundless sea, come to this? I cough, and feel something wet splutter onto my chin.

A sudden harsh scream brings my attention back to the present. Madame Loubrette is flung through the open doorway, sailing over my head and coming to a harsh landing on the driveway just beyond my field of vision. They found her, then, I think. Down there in the cellars. Down there in the dark.

There is another flash of movement and I realise that the Prussian has returned. It takes a moment for me to recognise him, due to the streaks of blood running through his hair and smeared across his face. He looks like a newborn.

'A little fresh air!' he shouts. 'To brush away the cobwebs.'

Madame Loubrette screams as Grost sits next to me. There is a hissing noise, then a soft punching sound, like the breath of a large pair of bellows.

'Ah,' says Grost, 'she's a pure-breed nightwalker! Thought as much: who wants to live in a cellar unless they have to? All those spiders and . . . Those little things . . .' He waggles his fingers at his mouth, miming 'horrible thing' like you would to a baby in its cot. 'What do you call them? Live under rocks. And in miserable cellars. Never mind. Doesn't matter, point is you wouldn't want to live with them, would you?' The screaming continues, getting harsher, as if Madame Loubrette is short of breath. 'Makes it much easier from our point of view – very short fight. You never can tell, though: sometimes sunlight kills them, sometimes it just makes them angry. Sometimes . . .' He looks down and smiles at me as if we're old friends. 'You won't believe this but I swear I saw it with my own two eyes – sometimes sunlight has no effect at all. Kronos and I once stumbled upon a bloodsucker actually sitting out

9

in the midday heat. He was getting a tan! The ladies do so like a tan . . .'

A smell of burning meat and hair wafts over and I briefly wonder if I'm hallucinating. Dreaming of the dark days of a couple of years ago when the Witchfinder was about his business. Then Grost's words make sense and I realise what must be happening to Madame Loubrette.

'Talking of tans,' says Grost, 'she's darkening wonderfully. I give her two minutes before she's as crisp as an autumn leaf.'

I try and speak again, but the fragile breath builds into a harsh cough and once more bloody phlegm splatters my chin.

'Try and relax,' Grost says. 'Soon be over.'

There is one final scream from Madame Loubrette. I close my eyes. I am cold.

'Next time,' says Grost, in a voice that now seems to be coming from miles away, 'because you never can tell with God, maybe there will be a next time . . .' I try and hold onto these words, as if they're coins dropping through my fingers, or sand pouring from the open hands of a young boy as he listens to the sounds of sails flapping in the wind. 'Try and make better choices. In my experience, we tend to get what we deserve.'

Oh God, I think, this is it, I'm dying . . .

'Who's your friend?' the Prussian asks, wiping at the blood on his brow before it drips into his eyes.

Grost shrugs. 'I didn't think to ask his name.'

I feel his fingers pulling down my eyelids.

Wait! I think. I'm not dead yet! My name is . . .

Four

Having dispatched the voracious Madame Loubrette, Kronos and I made our return to the road. Though perhaps that infers a more equal arrangement for the driving than has ever existed between us. If so, let me be quite clear: the division of labour is a very simple one – he kills things, I do everything else.

Some have assumed that I would resent the one-sided nature of our arrangement. Not at all. Kronos really is exceptionally good at killing things, much better than I am. (I'm squeamish and have the lousy habit of pulling back at the last minute, which only drags out the messy business and puts me in danger.) Killing things is incredibly tiring work, though, and he needs to conserve his strength for the task. Equally, I am much more practical in the day-to-day minutiae of life on the road. I can cook, I can sew, I'm good at fixing things. If our roles were reversed, gentle reader, you could be sure that not only would I be delivered unto the arms of a despairing God within moments of facing a vampire, but also the horses would not be well-fed and the dinner

11

would be late and very disgusting. We have our individual strengths in life: only an idiot goes against them.

So I sit up front, encouraging the horses to greater speed along the ill-tended roads of our country while Kronos rests in the back, dreaming butcher's-shop dreams.

I have seen a good deal of our country from the seat of that coach, and have the bruises on my rump to prove it. The major drawback of our lifestyle is the way we never seem to stay in one place. All those nights wrapped in a blanket on the earth, with the stars for a ceiling. Ah . . . but though it sounds romantic, it is not! It is damned uncomfortable and I would gladly never see a star again if it meant that I might be guaranteed a soft mattress every night. Despite the shape of my back I am not – as I frequently tell Kronos – a tortoise. I do not carry my home with me.

Actually, most people assume that Kronos and I are completely unburdened with such a comfort as a house. They can't imagine us in such conventional terms, I suppose. This is not true: we share a perfectly nice place just outside Stratford-upon-Avon. It's an old stables and lovely. In fact, it's quite the nicest house I have ever made an effort not to spend any time in. Between 'missions' – should there ever be such a luxury as 'between' – it stands there for our use. Sometimes we have spent as long as three days in it.

This – hooray for small mercies – is to be one of those occasions when we will visit. Madame Loubrette's academy was only a few hours' drive away so it would have been foolish not to aim the coach there. I made for the house's beds and roof with the sort of enthusiasm normally only felt by a mule for a good lie-down.

It was evening when I hit the banks of the Avon and urged the horses along that last, familiar stretch. By the time I pulled up the driveway and into the small court-yard the moon was up and the shadows were thick.

I banged on the side of the carriage after loading my flintlock pistol and yanking the heavy silver cross I wear around my neck from beneath my shirt so that it glinted in the fading light. The problem with a vampire hunter owning a house, of course, is that it means the bastards have somewhere to lie in wait for you should they be lucky enough to get your address. When I bemoan the irregularity of our time there it is this point that Kronos always labours.

'I put myself in danger every day,' he says in that slightly stilted tone of his. 'But why put your head in a noose for the hell of it?' This is usually followed by my having to build a campfire and hunt for a rabbit to cook on it. But not tonight.

'Keep your wits about you!' I shouted. 'We're home.'

The carriage door creaked open. 'My wits are always sharp,' Kronos replied. I caught a whiff of hashish smoke on the breeze and sighed. He insisted that the drug didn't slow his reaction speed but I knew the untruth of this. He found it helped him to relax but of course it took the edge off his abilities. And occasionally it dulled his reason. Vampire hunters should not giggle at everything, that has always been my feeling on the matter. I cocked my pistol.

'Perhaps I had better go first,' I suggested.

Just as I was stepping down there came a noise from the darkness and I was aware of Kronos leaping over me and plunging into the shadows to draw out whatever unwelcome visitor lurked on our porch.

'Oi!' came a young man's voice. 'You trying to kill me?'

Of course he is, I thought. In fact, you can tell he's not on form by the fact that you've had time to ask!

The young man was pushed out into what was left of the daylight. He slipped in the dusty earth and fell to his knees. 'Hey,' he said holding up his gloved hands. (He's a horseman, I noted as I took in his boots and breeches.) 'I just fell asleep – didn't mean nothing by it! I saw there was nobody home and thought I'd rest awhile. No crime, is it?'

'It is if you do it in another man's home,' said Kronos, pressing the tip of his sword against the young man's throat. 'Do you see an inn sign hanging anywhere?'

'No, no . . . look, in my job you take your rest where you find it. Your porch was shaded and it beat lying in a ditch for another night.'

'What is this job of yours,' I asked, 'which has you so well paid that you spend the night in ditches?'

'I'm a messenger, sir,' he said, 'since the war . . . and, well, you take your night's sleep where you can find it.'

You and me both, I thought. 'You have a message for us?' I asked.

'If either of you is Kronos.'

'That would be the man about to open you a new air hole.'

'If you are a messenger,' said Kronos, 'where is your horse?'

The young man looked uncomfortable for a moment, then decided that telling the truth could hardly put him in a worse position. 'In the stables,' he admitted. Kronos gave a chuckle and, with a whistle of steel cutting through the air, he replaced his sword in its scabbard. 'Hand over your message,' he said, 'and then you had better join your mount. I am not such an unreasonable man as to deprive a man of shelter, even one who has the cheek to help himself to it rather than ask politely.'

The relief on the young man's face was palpable, even in the dimming light. He was half giggling with nerves as he pulled a letter from within his jerkin and handed it over. 'Thank you, sir,' he said. 'You're too kind.'

'Yes,' Kronos replied, with a dreamy smile. 'I am.'

He unfolded the letter while I unhitched the horses. The messenger – knowing when he was onto a good thing and determined to keep it that way – helped me. We led them into the stables and tethered them along - side their new visitor. Even horses deserve to be sociable once in a while, I decided. I wonder if they share stories of the open road and the particularly fat people they have been forced to carry?

The coach was pulled inside too and I made sure it was locked. I was only too happy to have a guest for the night but I knew better than to be careless of security: if the messenger saw what was inside we'd find it hard to explain. That done, I told the young man he'd be welcome to food once I'd got around to cooking it and then I left him to his own devices.

Outside, Kronos had lit a couple of lanterns on the porch and was sitting there, smoking and staring up at the brightening stars.

'Tomorrow we ride south,' he announced, holding the letter out to me.

I sighed. Yes, of course we would . . .

Five

A Letter from Dr Ambril Marcus

Kronos,

I hope this finds you well. In truth, I hope it finds you at all. If only half of what I have heard over the last few years is true then you are a busy man. And I thought our retirement from the army was to have brought us easier lives! Ah, but soldiers never really retire, do they? We just wait for our next battle.

I've done my waiting here in a small village called Padbury, just north of Letchworth. I took what I learned on the battlefields and became a local doctor. Such a position keeps a roof over my head even if most of my days are filled with complaints of ancient curses and of being placed under the evil eye of local witches. You know what people are like in the country – a touch of the vapours and they look to the devil.

Perhaps I should not joke, for certainly recent events make me wonder if there are infernal powers at work here. You will remember I prided myself – to the point of obstinacy! – on my rationalist beliefs. Many were those, driven mad by the blood they saw spilled in Ireland, who became delusional. You only have to listen to the stories of battlefield spirits, of the unearthly ring of steel on steel that lingers on those bloodied squares of earth, to realise that you're listening to a man driven mad by what he has seen. And yet . . . Kronos, I know you believe in creatures beyond the normal ken of man. I have heard tales of your mission across the countryside. (And beyond? I heard tell that you had spent several months in Wallachia.) I will confess I have been uncertain whether I could believe these reports. Not that I have anything less than the utmost trust in you – I'm sure you won't think that – but your adventures sound so fantastical.

Perhaps I'd better give you some background.

Padbury is a tiny place, no more than a collection of dwellings that cling to the skirts of Padbury Forest, an ancient spread of woodland that has provided for the locals for centuries. Most of them earn their living from the land, though we are also home to the Durward family seat. You will remember Hagen, of course?

The closest family to me are the Sorrells who live just a short walk from my home. I have tended to their health many times – most especially through the harsh winter of two years ago when George lost his wife and the children found themselves without a mother. They are good, God-fearing people and their youngest, Ann, is not a girl inclined to over-imagination, a factor which is vitally important in the story I have to relate.

I was returning from a visit to a nearby patient, an obese old farmer who seems entirely filled with beer, I swear he makes sloshing noise when he walks. Cutting through the woods, I came across Ann standing in the middle of a small clearing. Her face was blank, her eyes unblinking. I thought she was suffering from sleeping sickness: I have seen such things before, people who wander while their brain is not yet engaged. Despite repeated calls I couldn't break through her dreamlike state. Eventually, following her gaze, I saw she was staring at a young friend of hers, Petra Wilkins from the other side of the forest. A beautiful girl, long blonde hair and the prettiest laugh you ever heard. Often I have seen the two together and wondered about the hearts they would go on to break.

(Why is Marcus going on about this stupid girl, you are no doubt thinking . . . Patience, Kronos, the point will soon become clear.)

As I drew closer, I realised I had been mistaken. Though the dress had been familiar, a pretty thing of cornflower blue, this was not Petra. Could not be. The woman in front of me was ancient, her skin so thin and fragile that it could have been spun by a spider. The hair that I had believed, when it caught the light, to be light blonde, was in fact white and so thin and brittle that it looked like it might have taken off in the wind, like the seeds of a dandelion. Her eyes were the right colour but the light blue – so like her dress – was hidden beneath thick cataracts. She reached for me, as if in need of assistance, long fingers coated with brown spots stretching towards me, the skin of her forearms hanging off the bone, swinging in the air, empty of muscle or strength.

You know, Kronos, that I have seen much in my life that has made me sick to my very soul. Yet I have always stood my ground. Looking at that woman, so old as to surely be beyond natural death, an animated corpse, not a thing who should be breathing . . . I felt a real sense of terror. Just for a moment I was horrified that her fingers – those chipped, yellow, nails – should touch me. It shames me to admit this, but I must convey the feeling. Unless I tell you the worst I can ask nothing of you. And you must come here, Kronos, you must. But when you do I shall at least know I have prepared you as well as I can.

I stood back, damn me for it, moving away from her touch. She spoke, and when the sound came it was with the fragile croak of last words, that rattle in the chest that can bring nothing but death.

'Doctor?' she asked, and it was as if the word itself was enough to break her. A trickle of blood ran from her mouth as it gaped open, the joint simply cracking and allowing her lower teeth to drop into the translucent cup of her jaw.

I made some form of exclamation – I cannot remember what it was. It would seem to have been loud enough to have shaken Ann from her dream (for I do not think she could have seen the terrible degeneration of the creature in front of me). She began screaming, a long, seemingly endless note that I could imagine would carry throughout the forest. The aged creature before me lost all cohesion, tumbling forward onto the soft earth with a delicate noise like the settling of cool ashes the morning after a grand fire. It was clear there was nothing I could do for her so I transferred my attention to Ann, gathering her up until she was calm enough to climb up on my horse.

I rode with her back to her home, leaving her in the care of her elder brother, Barton (an unfortunate fellow, half-lame but a devoted brother to Ann).

On returning to the clearing I found the aged unfortunate was in a bad way indeed. The body that lay in front of me had all the appearance of a cadaver that had been left in the open for some weeks. It was becoming part of the very ground beneath it, distinction between flesh and soil lost almost as I watched.

What manner of monster can wreak such damage? I only hope that you know of it, my friend. Moreover, I hope you know how it can be stopped.

Six

Barton Sorrell Is Always Falling

They joke about it down the tavern, they say 'It's not the falling that did for you, Barton, it was the landing.' I know what they mean and I suppose they're right. But at night, when the sleep don't come and the pain in my hip is like twenty hot coals, it's the falling I remember. It was when falling that I lost everything. It was when falling that I was out of control. It was when falling that I was weak.

All it took were a moment, the low sun in my eyes and a damn stupid thought that I could see the whole world from up there. Stupid. Can't see nothing from up there, nothing but my tiny life. Loose piece of roofing, foot skating like on the iced river in winter. Then the falling, the moment when it don't matter what you do, flapping your arms against the will of God. God don't care, I know that well enough now, He'll break you soon as look at you.

Now I need these stupid sticks to get me anywhere and if I were a horse then Pa would have shown sense and shot me in the back of the head.

Falling. And losing everything I had on the way down.

Dr Marcus was kind but I didn't want no kindness. I wanted my legs or I wanted nothing. I got nothing.

It's proven today, when Marcus brings my precious Ann to me. Crying she is, like she's heard the worst news in all the world.

'Look after her,' says Marcus, like I need to be told. I've been looking after Ann her whole life. 'Something happened in the forest, I don't know what.'

With that he rides back they way he came, leaving me with my sobbing sister and no idea how to make the tears go away.

'What is it, my love?' I ask her. 'What happened?'

'Petra,' she says, and I have to listen hard to under-stand the name through the tears. 'She came and took her.'

Petra was it? That stuck-up little sow. I'd like to say I was sorry but it would be a lie and a skill for lying was something else I lost when I fell off that roof. I've never understood what Ann sees in the girl and if she'd finally shown her true face, then – however sad Ann felt at the time – at least the lesson was learned. Petra was vain, stuck-up, treated people like they were lucky just to be in her company. Still, nobody seemed to see it. Wrapped everyone round her little finger she did. Including Ann.

'Who did she take?' I ask.

'Petra,' she says again and I give up on making sense of it. I want to lead her into the house, pick her up in my arms like I used to do when she was smaller. Can't do it now, not with these damned sticks. As it is, we lead each other. Maybe that's not so bad. Maybe it helps take her mind off Petra, worrying about me for a while.

Inside, Ann sits down at the table and I lean against the fireplace, sticks rested up against the grate.

'Tell me,' I say. 'Tell me everything that happened and I'll do my best to make it go away.'

'We were just sitting in the shade,' Ann says. 'I was brushing Petra's hair for her when I thought how beautiful she'd look with a few flowers woven in so I left her to go and fetch some.'

Beautiful? Aye, Petra was that. On the outside, at least. We all liked looking at her. She knew that much, of course, and played on it for all it was worth. Petra could get any man to do her bidding, *any man*.

'I wish you wouldn't dote on her so,' I say, 'acting like you're her handmaiden or something. You're twice the woman she is.'

Ann just looks at me, confused, and carries on talking.

'I went towards the river, thinking as how I'd seen some beautiful Lady's Mantle there. I didn't go far, just enough so as I couldn't see Petra any more. And I stood there, staring at the flowers, hearing the sound of the water and I knew . . .' Ann begins to cry again, the memory of it enough to set her back off.

'It's all right, my girl,' I say. 'You let it out, let it all out.'

'There was something there,' she says, her voice angry, fighting her own tears, 'I could feel it! Walking out there, its feet turning the ground to ash as it walked, just like Father Volk said during his sermon last week. The embodiment of evil! The devil himself!'

'Come now, girl,' I tell her. 'Don't go worrying about what Volk says – he just loves to scare people, is all, loves to keep them awake at nights. He don't mean nothing in what he says.'

'No!' she insists. 'It's all true! I felt him. I did! It was like I had become smaller than the eye could see, like looking down on myself. Out there in the shadows of the trees, lost I was, lost in all the ivy and the dead things that make the earth soft. I could hear them, Barton, I could hear the worms eating!'

Ann's breathing becomes laboured and it makes me think of Old Ma in those last few days, propped up in bed, chest making a noise like a dog in pain whenever she tried to drag one more breath inside her. It panics me to hear that and I hop over to my sister, holding her tight until she begins to calm down.

'That's it, girl,' I say. 'Whatever it was has gone now. Long gone. Get your breath and don't cry.'

After a moment or two she does. Holding onto the wood of the table as if she's scared she might fall off if she doesn't.

'I went back to Petra,' she says. 'To where I'd left her. And what I saw . . .'

Her stare goes somewhere else – looking inside her own head, I guess. It's a bang on the door that brings her round. She flinches as if whoever it is is hitting her and not the wood.

'Don't worry,' I say, 'I'll get it.'

I hop over to the fire, grab my sticks and, with their support, go and answer the door. It's Dr Marcus.

'How is she?' he asks, looking over my shoulder.

'Confused,' I answer, feeling – I don't know why – that I want him to leave so I can keep my sister to myself.

He nods. 'Can Isabella look after Ann for a bit? There's something I want to show you.'

'Isabella's not here,' I tell him. 'She's over in the fields helping Pa.' She's always helping, I think to myself: ever since the accident it's only me that sits around here all day.

The doctor thinks for a moment and then nods again towards his horse. 'Ann will be all right for a while. Come over for a minute.'

I don't like to leave Ann but she's still staring into space, and Marcus is walking across to his horse.

It feels like I have no choice and that makes my anger burn even hotter as I make my way after the doctor.

'She's had a terrible shock,' I say. 'I should be keeping an eye on her.'

'She'll be fine,' says Marcus. 'I'll make sure of that before I leave. First I want you to look at something for me.'

There is a sack hanging off his saddle. He pulls it down and unties the neck. Inside looks like nothing but earth, then the late sun catches something bright in there. He pulls it out. It's a short necklace, a plaited knot of silver at the end. I know it, of course, have seen it dozens of times.

'That's Petra's,' I say. 'Where did you find it?'

Dr Marcus nods and drops it back into the sack. 'With what's left of the poor girl,' he says and, while I'm looking into that sack of dirt, I find I recognise something else. A finger bone. And suddenly I'm falling all over again.

Seven

Carla Loves to Dance

My hair smells of egg and tomatoes. What a waste of good food.

Mind you, if I have to stay here much longer I'll be glad of it. Do you think a girl can survive by sucking her own hair? Knowing my luck, hair-sucking will be another offence against God (who I'm told frowns on most things) and I'll be beaten all over again. Not that I mind the beating so much. All you have to do is smile while it's happening and most men soon lose their stomach for it. The stocks, though, and the smell of sun-cooked egg – that's what I hate. My back feels like it's been folded in half after the first few hours. Come evening I know I won't be able to unbend if I try.

And all because I do so love to dance.

And what's so wrong about dancing, Sabbath or no?

Yes, it was in the churchyard. Yes, it would have been better had I not been with young Tom the coachman (but he is such a pretty young thing and the best dancer I know). Maybe it was the lack of clothes. But it was a lovely evening and clothes just get in the way when you're having a really good dance.

I try and get comfortable but all I get for my trouble is a tomato seed in the eye. I don't think I'll ever be able to eat a tomato again. This experience has put me right off them.

What's that? Hooves? Another traveller . . . I can still taste the last one. But then, he did try and burrow under my skirts and what did God give a girl teeth for if he didn't want her to defend herself?

This isn't just a man on horseback, though: the sound is too heavy. This is a coach. Which means that either my luck is improving or the day is about to get worse. This is about usual – I never seem to be able to enjoy a quiet life, things are either really good or really bad.

I spit out the mouthful of hair that I was currently enjoying and try and look up as the coach draws to a halt a few feet away. It's no good, I can't see a thing.

I hear the coach door open. Someone climbs out. The toes of a pair of boots move into my line of sight. They're very nice boots. I hope their owner deserves them.

'What are you in trouble for?' he asks, and his voice sounds foreign but is gentle. A good sign, not conclusive but enough to give a girl hope.

'Dancing on a Sunday,' I tell him.

There is a pause. I guess he's wondering whether to believe me or not. I don't altogether care. Who is he to judge me? Either he will try and take advantage of me while my hands are bound or he won't. Either I will have to kick him really hard or I won't.

Then he draws his sword and I realise that maybe I'll have to do more than kick him. The metal whistles through the air and I cry out as the stocks shake around my wrists and neck. What does the idiot think he's doing?

Then I realise that the stocks are no longer fastened. He has released me.

This doesn't mean I still won't have to kick him, of course, but it does mean I'm less inclined to do so. So far he's turned out to be my sort of man.

I open the stocks slowly and let them fall to the floor before carefully standing up and straightening my back. I really want to cry out – this hurts so much – but I don't. Never show a man you're hurting, that's what my mother told me and I've stood by it. I push my hair out of my eyes and take my first good look at him. He's nice, older than Tom but with the same long blond hair.

'Thank you,' I say, determined that we should at least try and set out on civilised ground.

He says nothing, just walks back to his carriage. Rude bugger.

Still, Carla, I say to myself, what you're looking at here is an opportunity. Do you want to go back to the village where they'll take one look at you before pelting you with spare food or do you want to find something better? My mother, as well as being a woman of sound advice, gave birth to no idiots. Life around here has consistently proved to be overrated. I run after him.

'Please?' I say, not quite sure how to ask.

He stops, half in, half out of his carriage. He closes the door slightly, not wanting me to see inside. Keep your secrets, I think, as long as I get a lift.

'We're heading east,' he says.

'East is good,' I reply.

He says nothing, just climbs inside his dark carriage and closes the door behind him.

'Come on,' says the driver, a small man with a tall hat and quite the sweetest eyes I've ever seen. He holds out his hand and helps me up beside him. He has a hump, I notice – it makes him sit awkwardly in the seat. I hope he doesn't catch me looking. I wouldn't want those eyes of his to turn sad.

'I am Professor Grost,' he says, holding out his hand. I take it. 'Professor?'

'I profess to be,' he replies with a chuckle before flicking the reins and driving the horses on. This is a joke he's told many times, I guess. Something to hide his awkwardness with strangers.

'And him?' I ask, indicating the carriage below and behind us.

'He is Kronos,' says Grost. 'And he loves picking up strays like you and me.'

I sniff at my dirty hair. 'My name's Carla,' I say, not that either of them had asked 'and I'm glad you stopped. I don't think I could have borne to stay there any longer.'

'Don't thank us until you know where we're going,' he says.

'East, he said.'

'Yes,' says Grost, with a smile. 'East.'

I can tell he's trying to be clever. Or funny. He's being neither but I feel no malice about it, he is not trying to be superior, he just isn't very good with strangers. We sit in silence for a while, driving further and further away from the village where I grew up. I am quite determined not to miss it. Since mother died it offers nothing but men telling me what they think I should do. They never succeed, and they certainly wouldn't approve of what I am doing now. Which is as good a reason as I can think of to keep doing it.

After a while the sky begins to darken and Grost looks for a place to sleep. It's all the same to me, I decide, and tell him so. We've long since left my old home behind us and as long as there is somewhere soft to rest my head I don't much care where it is.

Eventually Grost settles on a clearing that offers shelter but also enough light for us to see what we're doing as we build a fire.

Even though we have stopped for a few minutes, the coach door stays closed and Kronos is hidden. This angers me and I head over there to force him out.

'No,' says Grost, grasping my wrist. He is seemingly only too aware of my intentions, despite my not having stated them out loud. 'He stays in there. That's that.'

'What makes him so special?' I ask.

Grost smiles. 'You'll see soon enough, I'm sure. Until then don't worry about it – just help me get this fire lit.'

He goes back to the rear of the coach where he pulls out food to cook on the fire. I stare at the dark windows. My saviour is quite mad, I decide. Perhaps I have been a little foolish to throw in my lot with the pair of them. Oh well, foolishness is a hobby with me and it hasn't killed me yet.

Once the fire is burning and Grost has strung a small pan of ingredients over it to stew, we sit down and he tells me a little about themselves. They travel a great deal, he says, up and down the country (and sometimes beyond). Kronos used to be a soldier, but Grost makes it sound like he still is. Though it's certainly not the Irish he's fighting. Perhaps he's a mercenary? I ask.

'No,' says Grost. 'Not in the sense you mean, anyway. Though we do sometimes get paid for our work. Or take what we want from those who have no more need of money.'

I must look concerned at that as he shakes his head and a look of panic crosses his face.

'That didn't come out right,' he insists. 'We're not thieves . . .'

'Why should I care if you are?' I ask. 'I have nothing to steal.'

'Nonetheless,' he says, 'we're not thieves. Or mercenaries.'

'You tell me lots of things you're not,' I say, 'when it would be much simpler just to tell me what you are.'

'You'd think so,' he agrees as he stirs the stew with a stick, 'but people tend to react badly when I do that.'

'I'm not like other people.'

'No,' he nods, 'Nobody ever thinks they are. Still . . .'

The coach door opens and Kronos steps out. He has a dreamy look about him, as if he has only just woken up.

'We are vampire hunters,' he says. 'Is dinner ready?'

Eight

Barton Counts Himself to Sleep

Ann doesn't ask me about the doctor's business outside and I see no good reason to tell her. He gives her a quick examination, his voice all soft like honey. He's a charming man, that Dr Marcus, I'll give him that.

'There's nothing wrong with her that sleep won't fix,' he tells me. 'Her nerves need time to settle.'

He takes his leave and I sit down with Ann to wait for the others to come in from the fields.

Now that the tears have stopped she seems to be half asleep, her voice all on one note as she wonders what happened to her friend. It takes me a while but eventually I realise she's forgot. I don't know what to do or say to that, seeing her young face all confused as she stares out the window.

'I wonder when Petra will come back,' she says. 'It'll be dark soon and she won't want to be in the woods then, not when the moon is out.'

'She'll be fine,' I say in the end, deciding it's better to play along than to correct her.

Eventually Pa and Isabella return and I tell them

what's been going on, I don't want Ann listening, though – I don't want her to hear what I saw in that sack the doctor carried. She makes life easy for me.

'I'm tired,' she says. 'Probably got too excited. What with Petra and the sun, and my birthday.'

Her birthday. It's tomorrow, something I had forgotten and wish she hadn't remembered. How are we to pretend that everything's all right?

'Aye, love,' says Pa. 'You get to sleep – don't want to spoil your day tomorrow, now, do you?'

I give him a look of disgust at that but I realise it's different for him and Isabella: they didn't see what was in that sack. I do my best to describe it once Ann has gone to sleep.

'But surely you imagined it,' says Isabella and that's the one thing likely to get my fury up. She's treating me like a stupid girl. This is what happens when you're forced to give up who you are: people forget who you were.

'I'm not one to imagine things, sister,' I tell her, 'If I tell you that's what I saw then that's what were in the sack and you can accept it as if you saw it yourself.'

'Sorry my love,' she says, knowing she's gone too far, 'but you've got to admit it's a lot to believe. Petra rotted away before his eyes?'

'I've heard worse,' says Pa, throwing another log on the fire as if it can help banish the darkness in his words as well as the darkness in the house. 'There's things out in those woods that would make God Himself afeared.'

'Oh hush with your scared talk, father,' says Isabella, never one to believe in something she can't hold in her hands. 'You've no more seen anything out there than I have.'

'I've heard tales,' he says. And he's right, too, as much as I don't want to admit that there might be something in it. There's always been those who say the forest is dangerous.

'Aye, and you remember what mother used to say: "There ain't no tale without ale."' She looks over to where Ann is sleeping. 'For her sake we'll have no more about it. The doctor didn't say it were catching . . .'

'The doctor didn't say a bloody thing!' I reply, getting a little tired of being told what to do by my younger sister.

'Well, that proves it, then,' says Isabella, always quick to keep on top in an argument. 'If there had been something to worry about he would have said, wouldn't he? He wouldn't let us all die of it.'

'That's true,' says Pa (and how I wish all the fight hadn't been knocked out of him when Ma died).

'It would be a different story if you'd been here, not me,' I say. 'If you'd seen the muck in that sack . . .'

'Maybe,' Isabella agrees. 'And maybe sitting here all day is starting to make you imagine things.'

I actually clench my fist at that. I'm seconds away from striking out at my own flesh and blood. It's not enough that I have to lose my legs, I have to lose their bloody respect and all. Pa sees how angry I am and steps between us.

'Now then,' he says, 'we won't have none of this. There's no falling-out in this family – we stick together like always. I dare say Isabella's right . . .' I make to

35

interrupt but he holds up his hand. 'Whatever the truth of it there's nothing can be done now. We'll have a nice day for Ann tomorrow and everything will be as normal as can be. She's had a bad time of it and she needs her family by her.'

Both Isabella and I nod at this. He's right and we know it. It don't stop the anger, though, so I go outside for a smoke.

Out in the cool air I begin to wonder if Isabella is right after all. It's so quiet and calm that it's hard to believe there could be anything in the dark to harm us. I take a slow pipe and try and breathe the anger out with the smoke. I've always had a temper on me and it's the one thing that got stronger after I fell. I need to fight it, I know that: it does no good raging away at family and friends. God, how I wish I could burn cooler.

That night I lie in my cot and try to think about anything but the sight of that finger bone, all gnarled and flaking like a branch taken from the fire. It's the sort of thing that keeps a man from sleep, that is. The sort of thing a man can't help but imagine as his own, however much he holds his hands up in the moonlight to count carefully.

Next morning and Ann is bright as summer, as if the night's sleep has washed away all memory of the day before.

'Look!' she says to me, holding up her wrist to show off the silver bracelet that Pa's given her. 'Isn't it beautiful?'

It is. As beautiful as it were on Ma's wrist. I remember how it caught the light as she lay dead in her sickbed, the only sign of life in a room of death. 'Aye, sister,' I say. 'But not as beautiful as you.'

Ann sticks out her tongue at me and for a moment it feels like we're both children again, chasing around our mother's skirts, me yanking her hair, her running off to tell.

'I'm going to go and show Petra!' she says and runs out of the house.

What to say? I call after her but her head's full of summer air and sunshine and she doesn't hear me. I reach for my sticks but I wouldn't get further than a few feet after her at that speed. Damn it!

'Let her go,' says Pa. I look at him and he's sitting in a single beam of light from the rear window. It shows up the tears on his cheeks. 'She's so like her,' he says. I don't have to ask who he means.

Isabella don't know where to put herself. I can see the awkwardness in her as she wrings her hands and looks from Pa to me and then to the open door through which Ann has just left. I realise then that half her bloody problem is that she thinks she has to replace Ma, to become the bridge between us all. That's what puts her in such a righteous mood half the time. I shouldn't be angered by it. And right then I'm not.

'Come here, sister,' I say, holding my arms wide. She comes to me. I hold her for a moment, before letting her go so that she can see to Pa.

I make my way outside to sit and wait for Ann to come back.

Nine

Carla Listens to the Night

And, of course, there's nowhere for Carla to sleep, is there? Oh no. And far be it from me to complain, because a vampire hunter needs his sleep and I should just be grateful they rescued me when they did. Vampire hunter. Oh dear. Carla, my girl, you have once again found yourself in the company of some very mad gentlemen. My mother always used to say: 'Carla, I don't know how you do it but if there's a wet brain hereabouts you'll find it. Moreover, you'll probably ask for my permission to marry it.' Not that I need her permission any more, of course. Nor do I want to marry them. Either of them. Even if one of them has got lovely hair and looks like he could wrestle a horse to death.

No.

Too mad.

Apparently they've been doing this for years, travelling up and down the country killing 'creatures of sin' wherever they find them. I'm lucky he didn't chop my head off when he had the opportunity, I suppose.

On the back of the coach are several large cases of equipment. They say that you can never tell what will kill a vampire, so you bring as many possible weapons as you can and hope for the best. There are crossbows, swords, enough crucifixes to make a priest weep with joy and several bottles of water that Grost tells me have been blessed. I suspect this is enough to have both of them hanged under the laws of the Lord Protector.

'We have worse worms than Cromwell to fear,' says Grost. Kronos just smiles. He is not one for talking. For a while I wonder if this is because he doesn't speak good English. His accent is clearly foreign. (I've lived in a village all my life and the strangest thing I ever saw was a dog with three legs – don't ask me what sort of accent Kronos's is, all I can tell you is that it's 'foreign'.) As we ate our meal, though, I decided he could speak English perfectly well – he just didn't have anything he wanted to say. That's all right: I like a silent man. Tom used to talk too much and men do get ever so upset when you stop listening. Better for all if they say very little to begin with.

After eating some of Grost's stew (which smells like my hair but tastes a lot better), I walk to a nearby stream where I can wash away the remaining traces of my elders' disapproval. The water is cold and it makes my head ache, though not as much as the stocks did so I guess it's an improvement.

Back at the camp, Kronos is sitting on his own. His manner makes it perfectly clear he would like it to stay that way.

'Your friend is not good company,' I say to Grost.

'Luckily for you,' he says, '*I* am!'

And this is true: he tells stories of their adventures together and, whether I believe them or not, they're exciting and funny. By the time we go to sleep I'm almost relaxed. Then I find out that I have nothing to sleep on but the earth and my mood sours. And from there on the night just gets worse.

Grost snores. He snores so loudly that he must terrify the wildlife. Certainly they can no more sleep than I can. They make that quite plain. At some volume.

It's not good to lie awake in the middle of nowhere with two lunatics close by. Try as you might to keep it at bay, it's not long before panic sets in. Anyone who has ever spent any time miles away from anywhere will probably know this but I hadn't thought about it before: where people *aren't*, animals *are*. There is nothing peaceful about a night away from civilisation. It barks, hoots, growls, buzzes and whines.

As if that weren't enough I begin to really think about my companions – the foreigner and the hunchback. Did I really expect to last more than a couple of days in their company? How stupid had I been to leave my home behind on a whim?

Growing up it hadn't been so bad. My mother had been the perfect cushion between the self-important attitudes of others and the playfulness of a child. But after Hopkins and Stearne . . .

Now is not the time to think of that. I have enough trouble sleeping without conjuring up images of those old bastards.

Too late. I am now well and truly awake, angry and

afraid, and determined not to suffer another minute of it.

I get to my feet and decide to head for the stream. The moon is full and I can see well enough. I get to the water and decide to turn right for no other reason than it being far too late to start planning ahead now. I figure that I'll walk a little way and end up finding some other people. Follow a stream or a river for long enough and you can't help but stumble on someone or other. I hope they're not mad next time.

Something screeches directly above me and I yell. I cannot tell you how much that annoys me. I am not a foolish girl who screams at the first sign of something alarming. Still, it startled me and you can't always help these things.

I look up but of course can't see anything. Bright as it is it's still not light enough to see far.

I decide it's just another of the stupid noisy creatures that have made it their mission to annoy me.

It screeches again but this time I feel something yank at my hair and I could swear it's a pair of fingers, reaching down from a branch to snatch at me as I pass. I turn and shout, determined to show whoever it is that they'll have a fight on their hands. I stand still for a moment, looking up into the branches above me. There's nothing there.

This is getting more than annoying.

I carry on walking and, with the predictability of every campfire tale that has ever been told, the noise returns as something moves through the air above me. I try not to picture what it might be, try not to imagine a creature with impossibly long arms and legs, dragging its way through the branches in pursuit of its night's meal. I try not to do that.

There is a high-pitched squeal and I begin to run, careless of whether I crash into a tree or not. Better that than just to stand still, getting more and more afraid.

There is a whipping sound – something passing through the air behind me – and then that scream again. I turn to look and see a dark shape fall to the ground.

'Best not to wander off,' says Kronos, standing some distance away, a crossbow in his hand. 'There's worse out here than bats.'

'Bats?' I look at the dead shape that he has shot out of the air. It is indeed a bat, a particularly large one. 'That's not a—'

'It's a bat,' he says. 'A species of flying rat that some-times likes to drink the blood of passing simpletons. Now come back to camp and go to sleep.'

Kronos walks off.

I am furious enough at his arrogance that I nearly continue in the opposite direction. Common sense gets the better of anger, though, and, after giving the dead bat an unfriendly kick, I follow the vampire hunter at a distance.

Ten

Barton Sorrell Hits the Bottom

When Ann doesn't return, Pa and Isabella head out into the forest to find her. They both walk the paths in widening circles, getting more and more desperate when she isn't found.

'Stupid,' Isabella says. 'Shouldn't have let her just wander off like that.'

'She knows these woods like the back of her hand,' I say. 'She'll be fine.' I'm lying to both of us, and I don't think she believes me any more than I do.

Ann was clearly not herself when she went running off. Who knows what might have happened to her? If she stumbled on the place where Petra died might she not have lost her mind? Run screaming into the trees only to get utterly lost? Isabella is right: I should have stopped her somehow. We all should have.

'I can't believe I've lost her too,' says Pa. He's been wandering around in a daze all day. He's not been right since Ma died but this is much worse than normal, like he's as lost inside his own head as poor Ann is out in those trees.

I often worry about what is to happen with my father.

He gets weaker with every passing month, as if he's slowly given up on everything he used to fight for. I can understand that he misses Ma, we all do, but in the end you have to look to those who are still alive, not just those who aren't.

It's early afternoon by the time Ann reappears. We're all gathered on the front porch, trying to decided what to do for the best, when Isabella catches sight of her at the forest edge.

'There she is!' Isabella cries. She jumps off the porch and runs towards her sister.

Pa just stares, sitting in his rocking chair, not quite believing his eyes, having convinced himself that Ann was gone for good. 'Ann?' he asks, in a quavering confused voice.

The sun's in our eyes and we can't see well. Ann is in silhouette as she walks towards us. Still, there is something strange in the way she moves. She is walking like me. Like someone who has fallen.

Isabella suddenly stops, letting out a brief cry.

'Oh God,' she says. 'Ann?'

I grab my sticks and move as fast as I can, dragging myself over the sun-baked earth and through the long yellow grass. I have to see, I have to help . . .

I lose my balance, trying to move too fast, and fall to the ground, one of my sticks snapping as I throw my weight on it wrong. I can't stop, won't stop, pulling myself along the ground.

'Ann!' I shout, as if I can knock the horror away through the sound of her name. 'Ann!'

She's still in silhouette as I look up but she falls

forward. Isabella tries to hold onto her but only manages to join us on the floor.

'Ann?' We're face to face, almost touching, but this isn't Ann. This is an old woman, older than any I have ever seen.

She opens her mouth to speak and her breath is sweetly rotten, like fruit left out to turn.

She reaches for me and that silver bracelet, which has now hung on the lifeless arms of two dead Sorrells, catches the sun so well that it burns my eyes.

'Ann!' I scream.

Eleven

Brothers in Blood – The Memoirs of Professor Herbert Grost: Volume One (Unpublished)

As always, I woke that morning fresh and full of vigour. What is the point of sleep, after all? It is just another one of those luxuries that illustrious professors and their vampire-slaughtering companions indulge in for no longer than necessary. Foolish sleep! Pernicious relaxation! Begone! Also, as deliriously comfortable as the ground is, a man can have too much of a good thing. The sooner he can get to his feet and rearrange what passes for his spine the better. Then there is the traveller's friend, bosom companion of all gentlemen of the road: breakfast.

Our new companion had clearly not slept well. When I woke her she had all the charm and sweetness of an ox in high summer. I left her to her unladylike language and threats of violence while I woke Kronos. He was not much better.

I tried to make cheerful conversation over the bread and ale but it was clearly beyond my companions and we returned to the road in a mood best described as 'surly'.

As the morning progressed, Carla thawed somewhat, asking me again about our exploits. This was perfectly normal, of course. It is easy to forget – steeped in this bizarre business as we are – that there are those who don't even believe in vampires. To Carla, announcing our vocation was as absurd as saying we were dragon slayers (though I've met one of those and I must say he seemed remarkably lucid). She would believe soon enough, I decided, if she were to keep us company in the days ahead.

I told her of our recent adventures with Madame Loubrette and of the business in the capital that I have referred to previously as the 'Affair of the Clerkenwell Count'. I mentioned our months overseas, following the trail of Dracula himself and his nest-partner Baron Vorshatis. They are marvellous adventures, thrilling to listen to. It certainly must be more fun hearing them than it was living them.

By the middle of the afternoon Padbury Forest was visible in the distance and Carla was more relaxed. I wasn't sure whether she believed a word I'd told her, but she had entered into the spirit of my stories and had enjoyed them for what they were.

In his letter, Marcus had said that the large expanse of trees was the hub of the local community, ringed by dwellings with a large enough gathering to the south for it to have earned itself the name Padbury Village. To the north was the large hall owned by the Durwards. It was Kronos who reminded me why the name was familiar.

Hagen Durward had been a commander in the New Model Army, famed not only for his tactical strengths but also his abilities as a fighter. The two are surprisingly rare to find in one man. A fine swordsman, he was feared and respected by his men in equal measure and he had led several particularly brutal campaigns in Ireland. It had been said that he was a man who would not brook criticism: the slightest difference of opinion was resolved by the sword. If you disagreed with him, Durward declared, then you would fight him and the victor's opinion would be the one that was upheld. So fierce was his reputation, so bloody and long the list of those he had slain in combat, that few chose to disagree with him about anything.

Once the fighting in Ireland was over, he resigned his commission to accept a peerage, settling here as Lord Durward to savour his memories of bloodstained steel. Such relaxation was to be short-lived: he contracted the plague two years later and died a typically agonising death. There were those who had served under him that still found themselves smiling to think of it today. He was not a man much loved.

We entered Padbury itself and Carla found the occa - sional confused stare more than she was comfortable with.

'Such is the way in parochial places like this,' I assured her. 'Drive a nice-looking coach through them and they think you're here to eat their children.'

'Oh,' she replied, 'I know what these places can be like. My village was no better. It's just the first time I've been on the other end of it.'

I shrugged. 'When you look like me you get used to impolite scrutiny. Let them talk – if that's all they have to entertain themselves with then life's a pretty miserable thing for them.'

The village was so small that it took us no time at all to be out the other side and skirting the edge of the forest.

'It's dark,' said Carla, peering between the trunks of the trees. 'I'm not surprised there's a monster in there.' She turned back and gave me a smile. It was a smile that suggested we both knew she was being silly. I didn't look forward to the time when she would be proven wrong.

We arrived at Marcus's house shortly after. It was a good size and I reflected that his medical practice must be relatively successful for him to be able to afford such a dwelling. Closer scrutiny showed that the living accommodation itself was remarkably small, the rest of the plot being taken up by outbuildings that presumably he rarely used. Perfect for us: we had plenty of space to store our tools away from the prying eyes of the locals, one of whom, a red-faced gentleman brandishing an axe, was there to greet us as we arrived.

For an awkward moment I assumed he must be Dr Marcus himself. But Kronos emerged from the coach and, ignoring the fellow, began to shout for his friend.

I gave the man a smile – I find this is good manners when someone is carrying heavy tools – though it wasn't returned.

Eventually, Marcus himself appeared. He looked far less intimidating than the red-faced fellow. Perhaps a little older than Kronos, he had a gentle, slightly studious-looking face and a mop of black hair that age had streaked white at the temples.

'He seems pleased to see us,' said Carla as she watched Kronos and Marcus laughing and patting each other on the back.

'Yes,' I replied. 'Unusual that, to be honest. Shall we unpack?'

Twelve

What the Beer Brought Out of Clyde Lorrimer

Now I'm not saying nothing. You know me, Clyde Lorrimer is a man to let matters be, he don't like sticking his nose into other people's business . . . If there's another word out of you, Bob Frimpton, I'll stove your head in with this here stool and to hell with the story . . . Well, mind you do . . . Mouth like a gaping arsehole when the plague's in town and just as likely to dump something of worth on us. As I say – and bloody well stand by, thank you very much – I am *not* a one for gossip.

But just you wait until I tell you what I saw roll up to Dr Marcus's place this evening.

I know there's some round these ways who don't hold much weight by the doctor's physick but I always say he did all right by my Mary so these newfangled leeches and powders is fine by me. Still, he knows some funny buggers, that's for sure and I wouldn't argue with anyone as says so.

I'm sorting out the wood for him, just finishing up as it's getting on and he don't pay me so well as I'm going to hang around all day. I've got a proper sweat on and

I'm looking forward to knocking it on the head with a quick drink – you know how it is.

All of a sudden there's this huge coach pulls in. Fancy-looking thing it is, windows all blacked out so as you can't catch a glimpse of who's on the inside. For a minute I'm thinking the Durwards have got themselves a new coach, then I figure that it isn't young Morris driving so it can't be. Sat there in the driver's seat is a hunchback and a girl. Yes, Frimpton, a hunchback . . . what about it?

Well, how do I know?

Of course he fit up there because I *saw* him, but he was a hunchback nonetheless . . .

What? Well, he bloody leaned forward, didn't he? I swear . . . one more word out of him and that's that, I'm not telling you all this for my own benefit am I?

Well, keep your bloody gob shut, then.

So, a hunchback – leaning forward so as he can fit – and a girl. Nice-looking girl, too, the sort that gets your britches sitting funny.

Aye aye, I think, what's going on here, then?

The coach pulls to a halt and the door opens. I'm thinking it's going to be some rich old toff, stopping off for a quick dose of salts or to have his stools stirred. They love all that, the rich ones, can't keep their bum-holes covered. Instead, this soldier steps out. Well, I assume he was a soldier, he had a soldier's jacket on . . . no, I didn't recognise the regiment, Luke, we're not all as obsessed with bloody soldiers as you . . . It was blue, with red bits on, doesn't matter . . . He takes one look at me and his hand drops to his sword. What have I done?

I wonders. Here I am minding my own business and some bugger's got an eye to running me through.

'Marcus,' he shouts and I can't say as he sounded like he was from this country, soldier or no. Remember that travelling salesman we had through here a few months back? The one with the glasses that made his eyes look the size of fly balls. Selling bottles of oil what he claimed would grow a leg back if'n it were hacked off by something. That's the one. Remember his funny voice? Kept sounding like he was going to start singing the words rather than speaking them? Aye, well, it weren't a lot like that but it was a bit. So he probably comes from somewhere nearby.

I don't *know* where the salesman came from, Luke. I don't know everything, do I? I'm just saying as this bloke's voice was funny like the other's was, that's all. Just giving an example.

So, I'm thinking some foreign brute's going to have me head off just because I happen to be between him and Marcus. Which don't seem entirely fair but, as I say, the doctor did well by my Mary and if I had to fight his side I would. And yes, Dudley, I did still have the axe in my hands, that's true, so I might not have done so bad.

'Marcus!' this fellow shouts again and that sword is out of its scabbard a little way and I'm thinking the doctor's upset somebody for sure.

'Dr Marcus lives here,' I said, which in hindsight weren't the cleverest thing to do if the poor old doctor had been hiding under the kitchen table waiting for this foreign killer to bugger off. Still, it were out now and you'd think the man would show me the time of day to at least acknowledge it, wouldn't you? Not a flicker.

'Marcus!' he shouts again as if I ain't said a word. Well now, manners like that you couldn't doubt he were foreign. They just don't know how to be civil, do they?

Well, yes, I suppose that salesman were all right but he was after something, weren't he?

Money, Luke, he were after your money.

I know you ain't got any but *he* didn't, did he? He just saw someone with all the brain of a dead hare and thought he'd try it on. Anyway, can I carry on? Too kind . . .

I'm wondering whether I'm going to have to put that there axe in the foreigner after all when behind me the door opens and the doctor's stood there, face like thunder. Oh Lord, thinks I, here we go.

Then, would you credit it, the pair sets eyes on one another and they're laughing fit to burst, running up to one another and hugging like a pair of girls. So I put my axe down, thinking that maybe it won't be needed after all which is just as well as the head on it's as blunt as a bull's pizzle and I'd have been pounding on 'em for half an hour afore they'd've lain still.

So Marcus and the foreigner goes into the house, still laughing, and I decide to see what's what with the other two.

The hunchback begins unloading from the back but not before I catch a glimpse of some of what they're carrying. They's got bunches of some plant or another, all tied up. I'm thinking it's medical, you know, seeing as they know the doctor, but the next thing I see is a bunch of sharpened wooden spikes. Now how would a sick man benefit from having one of those rammed in 'im, eh? And that's not all, there's a whole box filled with crucifixes, small ones, big ones, metal and wood. Either their the holiest folk I's ever met or there's something up.

'Who's your master, girl?' I ask the young woman, giving her a bit of the old Clyde charm, you know? You can tell she likes it, she looks me up and down, getting a proper eyeful. No, she didn't have to stand back! That's it . . . I'm not carrying on unless Frimpton pisses off, I have had more than I can stand! No. I warned you. That's that. No. Definitely not . . . why, thank you Bob, don't mind if I do, thirsty work all this talking.

So, where was I? That's right, the poor girl was just about falling in love with me after I'd asked who her master was.

'His name's Kronos,' she says, 'And he's not my master.'

Yeah, I know that could sound sort of like she was brushing me off but you had to be there. It was much more, sort of, like she fancied me. Anyway, she couldn't hang around, of course, so she carried on unpacking, leaving me there on my own by the coach.

Well, as I say, I'm a man who knows how to mind his own business but there was something up here so I thought as it was my duty to find out as much as I could. So, while the two of them were taking boxes into Marcus's stable I opened the door of the coach and took a little peek inside. I told you how the windows was all blacked out so it was difficult to see inside there. I didn't

want to swing the door wide open and get caught out –
I hadn't forgotten about the foreigner's sword and I was
damned if I was going to have my innards on the
cobbles for the sake of curiosity. One thing that hit me
straight away, though, was the smell. It don't matter
how fine the coach looked from the outside, inside it
smelled of damp and rot, like when the soil turns in
autumn.

I don't mind admitting I was of half a mind just to
close the door and leave well be. I wasn't sure I wanted
to set eyes on what might smell that bad. Still, thinking
of you lot, and of my duty to those hereabouts, I decided
to risk a quick peek. And thank the Lord I did for you'll
never believe what I clapped eyes on in there . . .

Whose round is it, by the way? Better get another one
in now, just to save time later, you know. What? It's all
right for you . . . you're not having to do all the talking.

So, inside that dark coach what do you think I saw,
eh? What do you think was the reason behind that low,
dank smell? I swear I am dying of thirst here . . . having
to recall the horrors I saw . . . why, thank you, Luke,
you're a gent, at least.

That's the stuff. Fair gets the tongue working again,
don't it? What's that? What was in the coach? Well, I'll
tell you right here and now: whoever this Kronos feller
is we may grow to regret the day he decided to visit
these parts. Inside that coach was . . .

Thirteen

Dr Marcus Breathes Easier

What a relief it is to have Kronos here at last.

I confess there were a number of times over the last few days when I had wondered whether I had been mistaken to call on him. A man feels such a fool when forced to admit he is out of his depth. Or perhaps it's just me . . . Still, there can be no shame in asking an expert when a situation arises that is outside the reach of your own skills. And nobody could doubt this was beyond the skills of anyone hereabouts. It was bad enough when it was just poor Petra, but when Ann was struck down too . . .

Oh . . . To look Barton in the eyes and admit that the same thing that had killed one must have killed the other. He hated me at that moment. And I can't say I blame him.

'You told me she was fine,' he said and I had, of course – I'd told him exactly that.

'I don't know what to say,' I admitted, 'but she was when I examined her, she was in perfect health. Whatever's doing this must have chanced upon her when she was in the forest.'

I could tell he'd been thinking the same thing. The animosity faded as he had his own suspicions confirmed and I went back to examining his sister.

Ann was by no means as badly affected as Petra had been. From what I could gather from Barton, she had retained enough strength after she was attacked to make her way home, falling at last once she was surrounded by those she trusted and loved. At least she died in company. There was no way Petra could have travelled that distance, though: when I had found her the act of talking had been more than enough to finish her. Either Ann was just naturally stronger or the attack on her had been less vicious.

I examined what was, to all intents and purposes, the body of an old woman. I might have been inclined to believe that the identification was a mistake were it not for the silver bracelet that hung loosely from her wrist. Her father explained that he had given it to Ann that very morning as a birthday present. Her birthday . . . How cruel God can be.

My thoughts turned to plague – as a medical man's often does these days. Was it possible that I was wrong in thinking they had been attacked? Was it not more likely that they were the victims of disease? A wasting disorder that withered the flesh on the bones? If so, I couldn't begin to know how to cure it. Should the Sorrells – and myself for that matter – be confined to our dwellings? Locked up with a red cross on the door to show that we were unclean? If that were the case then certainly it was a matter for me, not for Kronos. And yet . . .

And yet. Despite what might have been weighty evidence to the contrary I did not think it was a medical matter. If pressed for a reason, I could only think back to the sensation I had felt when I had noticed Ann standing there in the forest, transfixed by the fate of her friend. It had been an awareness of the unearthly, a taste of evil.

Many doctors lose sight of God and of affairs beyond the body. In their daily dealings with the worst corruption that flesh can attain they leave the notion of spirit behind. For me – while I have certainly seen sights so terrible that they will haunt me all my days – my work has done the opposite. I have seen the face of God reflected in the eyes of every dying man I have attended. I have seen the hand of God in every miraculous escape from death. I am a good doctor, I have saved many lives, but I have done so with God at my side.

And if one believes in God . . .

I left the Sorrells with all the apologies and commiserations I could offer and returned home. I hadn't dared hope that Kronos would arrive so swiftly and, when I heard the sound of a coach outside my door, I assumed it was a visiting patient. As much as it may be my livelihood I did not feel in the least bit inclined to offer a consultation.

Then I saw him, and the years had barely touched him – a surprise given the accounts I had heard of his lifestyle: I welcomed him with open arms and, as I looked at his face, I realised that he was not quite the same man I once knew. There was a darkness in his eyes, a look of pain that his smile, however broad, never quite touched.

I led him into the house and poured us both a glass of wine.

'I didn't imagine you would be here so soon,' I admit, once we are seated.

'You were lucky,' he says. 'We just happened to be passing our home for a night. Had you written any later it could have been months before we received your message.'

'Then fortune may be on my side after all, however much it may seem to the contrary.'

I tell Kronos all that I have seen, plus what I suspect and fear. It's a valuable experience to be able to let go of it all. Only by doing so do I realise quite how much I have let the weight of events bear me down.

'You know what it is that plagues you here,' he says, once I finish my story. 'Or you wouldn't have written to me.'

'I wrote to you because I needed to write to *someone*,' I tell him. 'There was nobody else that I could think of.'

Kronos smiles. 'You believe so many things without question,' he says. 'For example, in the power of your herbs to heal or your leeches to purify. And yet you will not believe the obvious facts that stare you in the face.'

'The tools of my trade are proven every time I save a life,' I reply. 'I don't give my belief without some evidence.'

'It's a vampire,' he replies, 'and I shall kill it for you.'

'A vampire . . .?'

I know of the legends, of course, and I have heard stories of my friend's work across the country. He is right that I suspected something of the sort. That trickle of blood from the mouth just before both girls died, that sense of evil . . .

'There are more types of vampire than you can imagine,' he says. 'Those who feed off blood, those that eat the flesh of a man or drain his sexual energy. I have even met a vampire who feeds off dreams, scaring its victims to death with visions so terrible that their souls cannot stand it.'

Kronos gets to his feet and looks out of the window where his friends are still unpacking their belongings.

'Here,' he continues, 'you have a vampire who feeds off youth itself, draining the life force from its victims and leaving them empty shells, like corn husks, cast aside.'

'It's unbelievable . . .' I say, though deep down I believe every word. How ridiculous it is, this fight between the head and the heart. Why must we always rage against what our instincts tell us?

'It's a fact, and like a wolf preying on a village it must be routed out and killed.' Kronos smiles. 'Lucky you know me, eh?'

Finally, his belongings are stored in the stable. I offer him rooms in the house but he insists they will be perfectly comfortable outdoors. I can tell that his companion, Grost, is somewhat saddened to hear this and resolve to ensure that he has my spare bed should he wish it. At least this will offer Kronos and Carla some privacy! It's explained to me that she is new to their party, having been collected en route, but if I know Kronos it will only be a matter of time. He always was a man of appetites and never seemed to have any difficulty in satisfying them.

We dine simply and Grost tells me stories of their time together – something he very much enjoys doing I can tell. Of course, I would like to think that his tales are subject to exaggeration but the events of the last few days rob me of that small comfort. So it is that, on retiring to bed, I am quite unable to sleep. Looking out of my window at the shadow of the forest, lit solely by the moon and the stars, it seems to me a place of horror. How many times have I ridden through those ancient trees? How often have I marvelled at their beauty? It now seems to me a wonder that I ever escaped the dark canopy with my life.

Sleep takes some time to come.

Fourteen

Carla Asks More Questions

Marcus seems nice. It will be good to help him. Some people follow their fathers into a livelihood, some just happen on a way of keeping food on the table. Marcus is different: his saving lives is important to him – you can tell by how much guilt he carries around. I wouldn't want to live like that. I have one person's death on my conscience and that is quite enough.

Kronos has decided that we can all sleep in the stables. Which is very gracious of him, I must say. Not that I'm uncomfortable, admittedly; the straw makes for a soft and warm resting place. Still, I would have liked the choice of a bed, as, I'm sure, would Grost. Marcus has invited him inside, I think, but he doesn't like to leave me alone with Kronos. Which is silly. I am perfectly capable of defending myself. Besides, Kronos sleeps in his coach as always – no bed of straw for him.

It would seem that we are on the trail of a vampire already. One that drains the life from women. I remark that we call one of those 'a husband' where I come from but nobody seems amused.

They take all this very seriously. While Kronos can

seem a bit full of himself I decide to rein in my inclination to mock for Grost's sake. I would not want him to think I was laughing at him.

'So,' I say to him, while we're completely failing to fall asleep, 'what happens now?'

'Well,' he replies, straightening the eye mask he likes to wear to keep out the light, 'now we have to try and track the creature. Most vampires masquerade as normal folk so it's a case of finding out who it is and then we can deal with them.'

'But surely it should be obvious? They can't walk around during the day, they have big teeth . . .'

'No, no, no,' Grost replies, waving his hands in the air. 'It's never that simple. Well, not often, anyway. Most vampires have an intolerance to sunlight, yes, but it's only a specific breed – a nightwalker – that can't step out in it altogether. Usually, with a bit of protection, say a hood or a cloak, they can teach themselves to endure it.'

'And the teeth?'

'Only bloodsuckers need fangs. From the sound of this type there's no need for it to puncture the neck so why would it have the tools to do so? Think about birds . . . some have long beaks so that they can poke them into the trunks of trees to feed on ants and beetles, some have short, sharp beaks to tear open the bellies of rats, some have spoonlike bills so that they can scoop fish from the sea. Nature gives you what you need.'

'But vampires aren't natural.'

'Well, that depends on your definition of natural, doesn't it? It's an animal that exists, just as we do. You can blame the devil for it, by all means, but that doesn't really help'

'But they're not born are, they?'

'No,' Grost answers. 'At least, I don't believe so. The condition spreads more like a disease. A disease that can alter the physical structure of the sufferer so that it can thrive. Ingenious, really.'

'You sound as if you approve.'

'Oh no!' He lifts his eye mask and looks over at me. 'They're the most terrible creatures you can imagine. There is a world of difference between being impressed by something and liking it. For instance, I think scorpions are amazing creatures – I wouldn't want one anywhere near me, though.'

'Fair enough,' I reply. Grost is so sweet when he gets worked up. 'So how do we plan on tracking it, then?'

'Ah,' he replies, 'that is rather difficult, it has to be said. There are a few methods that I'll happily show you tomorrow. The only sure way of getting your hands on a vampire, though, is to catch it in the act.'

'Oh,' I say, rather disappointed. 'That doesn't sound like the best plan I've ever heard.'

'No,' Grost admits, 'it can be somewhat awkward. You have to hope that you can catch the thing before it's killed everyone within sucking distance. Night-night.'

With that he pulls his eye mask back down and goes to sleep.

Fifteen

Marcus Pays His Respects

Today sees the funerals of both Ann Sorrell and Petra Wilkins and it is my unfortunate duty to attend both.

Leaving my guests to busy themselves with their own tasks, I ride through Padbury to the small church on its far side. When the building was originally constructed the graveyard was barely twenty feet square and the tiny plot soon filled up so that the gravediggers were forced to branch out, climbing a hill to the rear. This has resulted in inclined funerals and a selection of lopsided crosses silhouetted against the sky. Never underestimate the numbers of the dead – they will soon prove you wrong.

All this topographical inconvenience tends to mean that interments are shallow and services brief. This latter is strongly against the prefence of Father Volk, a particularly theatrical Puritan who likes nothing more than beating his congregation senseless with the blunt edge of his religious fervour. Some priests like to give their congregation a sense of love and awe, some just like to give them nightmares. Father Volk is of the second school.

'Ah.' His voice booms from within the shadows of the vestibule. 'Dr Marcus. I had wondered if we might have your company today.'

'Indeed you shall,' I reply. 'And why might you not?'

'Oh.' Volk dismisses the thought with a wave of his hand, as if trying to bat away a particularly intrusive horsefly. 'I wouldn't have blamed you for feeling unwelcome, considering. It can't be easy to be the man they turn to to keep the spectre of disease from the door . . . and then to fail. But then, none of us are perfect – except the Almighty.'

It is clear that he considers himself a close exception. Still, I choose not to comment on any imperfections we might possess.

'In both cases it was too late for me to assist.'

'Really? I understood you were present when Petra passed. And, of course, you spent time with poor Ann the day before she joined her friend in the heavenly fields.'

It is, of course, frowned upon to kill priests. I there-fore choose to continue ignoring Volk's remarks. It's safer that way.

He stares at me for a moment, then offers me a distinctly brutal smile and returns into the darkness of his church.

I walk over to where two holes have been freshly dug in the vertiginous graveyard. Young Luke Hopkins, gravedigger and preserver of the local tavern's fortunes, is sitting on the edge of the hole, dangling his legs inside and mopping at his sweating brow with his shirt-tail.

'Hot work,' he explains, as if it were necessary to do

so. 'Don't know why we're bothering for that Petra Wilkins either. From what I hear there ain't more than a bucketful of her to bury.'

'It's about the ritual,' I say, angry at his callousness.

'That may be so,' Luke replies. 'But there's no ritual that's going to put me back on my feet. Two graves in one morning – I ask you. Another five minutes and somebody would have had to dig a third.'

I decide that it's best to leave Luke to his recovery. Everyone I have met thus far seems designed to anger me. But then, Luke's attitude is not so unusual: how else can the young face death other than by dismissing or laughing at it? It's a time-honoured method and I shouldn't let it get to me. It's not as if Luke actually saw it happen, after all. That was a burden placed only on myself.

I notice Petra's family at the church gate and catch my breath for a moment. Is Volk right? Do they believe I have failed them in some way?

Saul Wilkins, Petra's father, is surprisingly small considering his trade as a blacksmith. He is also perpetually sweating, so that one wonders if he started off large and has simply been worn away over the years.

'Doctor,' he says, nodding at me. 'Good of you to come.'

'Not at all,' I say, bowing my head towards his wife.

Katherine Wilkins is not so polite. She stares at me for a moment, opens her mouth as if to speak and then shakes her head, moving past me and walking towards where Luke is still sitting in her daughter's intended place of rest.

'You'll forgive my wife, I'm sure,' says Saul. 'It's knocked her hard, as you would imagine.'

'Of course.'

'I don't suppose you have any more idea what it was . . .?' he asks, scratching at his short beard as if he's forgotten the rest of his sentence.

'I'm afraid not,'

'Only we'd heard you'd called for someone to come and help. A foreign gentleman, I believe?'

Even after all these years I forget how small a village really is. You simply cannot keep a secret in it.

'He's just an old friend,' I say, 'from my army days.'

'Oh aye . . .' Saul looks uncomfortable at that, as well he might had he ever seen Kronos fight. Stories of the violence wrought by the New Model Army in Ireland have made many folk wary of ex-soldiers. They're often quite right to be so.

'He's just visiting for a few days,' I continue. 'You have to look after your old comrades, don't you?'

'Of course,' Saul says, not having much choice but to agree. 'Of course you do.' He looks over to where his wife has begun arguing with Luke. The young man leaps out of the hole as quickly as if something inside it had grabbed his foot. 'I'd better . . .' He moves over to help whichever of them appears to need it most.

The rest of the village arrives in dribs and drabs. You don't bury someone in circumstances like these without drawing a crowd. Everyone wants to know what happened to these two girls, and if the villagers manage to catch a glimpse of their remains, all the better. Such ghoulishness is hard to understand but it will for ever be a part of human nature and there's no point fighting it. Standing in the shade of one of the trees I can hear stray pieces of conversation floating over on the light breeze.

'Like a woman of ninety, so I heard.'

'Crumbled away to nothing.'

'New type of plague.'

'The doctor will be next, most likely.'

'Foreign he is, turned up last night.'

I see the Sorrells making their slow way along the road. Barton can hardly help slowing them down. I notice that one of his crutches has been snapped and then fixed, which makes me picture him tumbling to the ground, coming face to face with his dying sister. He is a man who has suffered altogether too much. I decide to walk up to meet them – anything to get me away from the crowd and its gossip.

Isabella is the one to greet me, so like her mother and always the strongest of the three Sorrells. 'Doctor.' She nods, and offers much the same greeting as Saul Wilkins. 'Thank you for coming.'

Again I can say nothing other than 'Not at all.' We are, after all, just trading polite chat. I am no more wanted there than anyone else. Who wants to be at a funeral?

Barton certainly doesn't.

'Look at 'em all,' he says with disgust, staring at the gathered crowd. 'Loving every minute of it, I dare say.'

His face is bright red and his forehead is dripping with sweat. It's obvious that he's finding it extremely painful to move along. I open my mouth, about to suggest that I should take a look at him, see if there's anything I can do to help. Then it occurs to me how unlikely it is that my offer will be appreciated. Barton doesn't want sympathy, he just wants his sister and that wish is beyond the power of any of us to grant.

'Oh hush now, brother,' says Isabella. 'It's lovely that so many wanted to show their respects. Ann was well loved.'

'Balls,' Barton replies succinctly. 'They're just a bunch of nosy bastards.'

Isabella gives him a sharp look but he ignores her.

Throughout all this, George Sorrell seems in another world entirely. His eyes are glazed, his mouth slack, he might be about to fall asleep. He is not a man who grieves easily: he took the death of his wife terribly hard and this can only be worse. When a loved one grows ill you prepare yourself, you make your peace with the sad process as best you can. None of the Sorrells had had that advantage with Ann. No doubt they had imagined that she would outlive them all.

We enter the graveyard and the idle chatter stops as we force our way through to join Petra's family at the graveside.

'Good morning,' says Volk, reappearing from within the dark church. He looks up at the sun and it's as if the light is all a bit too much for such a dark soul as his. He squints and gives a great sigh as if unburdening himself of the most terrible weight.

'Let us abase ourselves in the sight of God,' he suggests, almost cheerfully. 'The all-merciful, the wise, the healer and the father.'

'Not that merciful,' someone mutters at the back and

Volk twitches as if there's a wasp at work beneath his robes.

'Silence,' he hisses. 'Have respect for the Almighty.'

Not to mention the memory of the two dead girls, I think.

'We are gathered here today to commit the bodies of Petra Wilkins and Ann Sorrell to the earth, to remember them as the bright children they were and to remind ourselves that only through firm obedience to God are any of us saved.'

I let his words drone away. I have no interest in the God of Father Volk: he is a prickly, cruel and vindictive God and not the one I believe in. Volk utters all the usual threats and contradictions and very little about the two girls we are here to remember. I decide to indulge in my own memories, casting my mind back to the years when I had been their doctor, smiling sadly at the thought of the beautiful and spirited people we have lost.

When the caskets are brought to the graveside, the families are united by their tears and I'm pleased to note a small fracture appear in George Sorrell's icy expression. He rubs his watering eyes and I feel relief that this important first step towards dealing with the death of a loved one is being taken.

Finally, Volk finishes his miserable litany and the caskets are lowered into their shallow holes. I take my turn to cast earth into the graves and privately wish the pair of girls all speed into the afterlife. Let it always be summer where you are, I think. May the sun never set.

As people began to file away I notice the Durwards' carriage pull off the road slightly. Paul Durward steps out. It's good that they've made an appearance, I think, albeit a late one. It's so rare that they leave Durward Hall these days and I don't think it has occurred to anyone to expect them.

Paul is holding a small wreath and I walk towards him, meaning to meet him halfway. He veers away, however, climbing up the hill towards the large tomb at its summit. It's then that I remember the date. It's the anniversary of his father's death: he's not here to attend the funeral of Ann and Petra at all.

I decide it's a perfect opportunity to reacquaint ourselves anyway and I climb up the hill after him.

Sixteen

Morris Blake Plans Ahead

Dearest Nell,

I am sorry it has been so long since my last letter but affairs in the Durward household have not been all they might be. 'When are they ever?' you will likely ask and I dare say you'd find nobody to disagree with you. Still, even for this hellish home, the atmosphere of late has been almost impossible to bear.

I have also been even more than usually cautious. I am under no illusion that they would be merciful should they find out that we're married. The mood here is so hostile that I would surely be beaten and hurled from the premises. How I wish I could understand this ridiculous notion that precludes a footman from taking a wife. I am living proof that it doesn't affect a man's work! I miss you, darling, but fear not: we won't be forced to live like this for ever. And yes, my dearest, I know it's hard on you too but where would we be if I didn't have this position? Our best hope is for me to make myself indispensable to the household and then, when I rise to the rank of butler, there will be opportunities for us.

So what of the household? Well, as you know, Lady Durward has long been a recluse. She sits in her chamber, barely moving. She might as well be as dead as her husband. If the glimpse I caught of her face the other day is any sign, she soon will be.

I had been ordered to accompany her ladyship and Master Paul to the grave of Lord Durward, it being seven years now since he passed. It was the first time she had left the house for nearly a year and she was dressed just as if it were old Hagen's funeral all over again. Head to toe in heavy black, layer upon layer of lace so that it was impossible to see her face. She moved at a slow crawl, as if every footstep had to be carefully considered before it was taken. It took great effort not to stare.

Master Paul helped her into the carriage and we drove to the graveyard.

On arrival, Master Paul stepped out and laid a wreath before the statue of his father. It is an impressive tomb, my love, and that's for sure: a stone Hagen looking down on all comers, twice the height of the real man but with that same terrible sneer the man wore in life. I dare say the worms have had that from him now. Just goes to show, we're all of us equal in the end. I know that sounds callous but I promise you he doesn't deserve consideration. Be glad you never met him, my love, he was a bastard right enough. (Forgive my language but there's no prettying the old man up.)

It's a wonder to me that these two could bring themselves to visit his graveside – you wouldn't catch me dead there if he'd been my relation. Unless, perhaps, I was in the mood for a dance!

Not that Lady Durward left the carriage, that job was Paul's alone. Still, I managed to catch a glimpse of her face. I was pushing the door closed when she leaned forward, noticing the approach of Dr Marcus – the medical man of hereabouts. She obviously still couldn't see well enough as, just as I was stepping back, she lifted her veil so as to look at him properly. It was a terrible shock!

Lady Durward had always been a fine-looking woman, one of those regal beauties, you know – pretty to look at but cold as ice. She had had, I suppose, all the warmth of her husband's statue. But good-looking for all that. No more! She has wasted away. The skin fair hung off her, great cream-white folds of it. It looked crisp and powdery, more like dust than flesh. Her eyes appeared utterly lifeless, little more than dark holes peering out from this goose-fat face. Perhaps she noticed me looking for she gave a low moan.

Of course, the noise might have had nothing to do with me, it might rather have been on account of her feelings towards Dr Marcus, feelings that were made only too clear when the man approached the coach.

'Forgive me,' he was saying, 'the anniversary had quite slipped my mind.'

'I wouldn't expect you to remember,' Master

Paul said, though not unkindly, just in that cool way he has. 'I am sure you cannot remember the deaths of every patient who has been in your care.'

'You would be surprised,' the doctor replied. 'Some of my profession develop a cold heart against death – I can't say that I have.'

'It is to your credit,' said the master. 'Though my mother would consider it of little compensation.'

'Paul,' the doctor said, 'you know there's nothing I could have done, the plague was too virulent . . . nobody could have saved him.'

'I know,' the master said, 'but my mother . . .'

I suppose the doctor caught a glance from Master Paul, for he suddenly realised that the lady in question was present. He glanced through the open door of the coach and he must have seen her face too as his look of keen embarrassment soon turned to one of horror. I'll give him his due, he was quick to cover it up with a gracious smile and a small bow.

'Lady Durward,' he said, 'I had no idea . . .'

'She won't speak to you,' insisted the master, leading him away from the carriage.

It got difficult to hear them but I could tell from the doctor's face that he was deeply concerned about what he had seen of her ladyship.

'It's the effect of the grief,' I heard the master say, and I reckon I believed that just about as much as Dr Marcus did. His expression was almost mocking as he led the master a little way further, no doubt wanting to ensure that Lady Durward couldn't hear what he was saying.

They had a brief but civil argument but Dr Marcus got nowhere and soon the master climbed back into the carriage and we left the doctor there.

Credit to Dr Marcus for caring, really. Had I been treated so dismissively by the lady in question I'm not sure I would work so hard to assist. Perhaps it was curiosity, too. I dare say that if I was a medical man I'd be fascinated by what could have brought about such a change in her ladyship. As it is, I try not to think about it: there can be little merit in my prying, I want to further myself, not end up out of a job.

On the subject of furthering myself, I very much hope that just such an opportunity is on hand.

I told you of how Mistress Sara always fusses around me, did I not? (And don't get jealous, my love! She's mad as a tramp's tick and not half the beauty you are.) She's a weird one and no mistake: you only have to watch how she and Master Paul carry on when they think nobody's looking, there's a way about them that just ain't natural. Anyway, she's always making eyes at me and I'm no fool: if she has a liking for what she sees then I'm not averse to turning that to our advantage. My only goal is, as always, for us to get enough money together to be safe, my love, and if the hardest thing I have to do is give the gentry a shy smile now and then I shall count myself lucky. This morning, just after breakfast, she hinted that there was something she wanted me to do for her and that I should find myself well rewarded for my efforts. That's what we like to hear!

In other news, the village gossip is reaching new heights. Two girls died last week and nobody seems to know what happened to them. Of course, that never stopped the owners of the chattering tongues from having a guess. From what I hear, their bodies were horribly aged – they'd wasted away before their loved ones' eyes. They should take a look at her ladyship! I bet she could give them a run for their money!

Also some strangers have arrived and they are staying with Dr Marcus, so I hear. One of them – a foreign gentleman – dresses like he's in the army and was seen wandering around the forest with several wooden boxes. Clyde Lorrimer, a man who it doesn't pay to believe too easily, reckons they were filled with . . .

Seventeen

Carla Learns The Trade

'Frogs?' I ask, not quite able to believe what I'm seeing.

'Toads, actually,' says Grost. 'Though, strictly speaking, there is no biological difference between the two. If it makes it any more palatable they're quite dead.'

'Toads,' I say, more to try the word out for size than through any real hope that it'll make sense. 'Dead toads.'

'Absolutely!' says Grost, dropping the floppy thing into a box and closing the lid. 'You see, it's like this . . .' He adopts a stance that is already only too familiar. Grost is a lovely man but he does so love to tell people things, whether they want to know them or not. 'If a vampire crosses the path of a dead toad, said amphibian will become reanimated. It will become a vampire toad, sucking the blood from other toads and generally being a terrifying nuisance.'

I stare at him. I think that perhaps he has completely lost his mind. In fact, if I watch long enough maybe it'll start pouring out of his ears.

'All right,' he admits, 'that last bit was a lie. They do come back to life, though.'

'Really?'

'Yes, really! It's a very useful method for identifying the presence of the undead.'

'Really?'

'Yes, *really*! Insufferable woman . . . I'll have you know I've been doing this for years – I do know what I'm doing, I hope you realise.'

'Who discovered it?' I ask.

'I beg your pardon?'

'Who realised that vampires bring toads back to life? And how? Did they just happen to have lots of dead toads lying around when a vampire came in and, all of a sudden, the toads were hopping around? And how come the vampire didn't kill the person concerned before he could pass on the amazing new fact that he'd discovered?'

'Yes,' says Grost, a little put out, 'well . . . a lot of what we know is somewhat anecdotal, passed down over the years. Who knows who first noticed the effect? The important thing is: it works. Now, are you going to help me dig or do I have to do it on my own?'

I smile. He's a sweet old thing and I wouldn't really want to upset him.

'I'll help,' I say. 'Sorry.'

Grost smiles back, and it's a lovely smile, soft and genuine. Not a type of smile I've seen that often. Back in the village where I grew up, people smiled when something bad had happened to someone else – or perhaps was just *about* to happen and they considered themselves lucky enough to be in a position to watch. Smiling was a sign of cruelty to come. It was not a nice village.

'Where do you come from?' I ask.

'Oh,' he sighs, 'I have moved round a great deal.'

Oh no, I think, I've set myself up for another long answer. As it happens, he surprises me:

'I don't think it's places that we come from, anyway,' Grost says. 'We are the children of history, not geography.' He squats down and begins to dig a hole. 'Though I suppose one could inform the other,' he continues, having thought about his own point a bit too much, as usual, 'if you lived somewhere horrid.'

'I did,' I admit. 'Really, really horrid.'

'Still,' he replies, 'I dare say it was the people rather than the place, wasn't it? The place itself was probably quite nice – it was the awful pigs living in it that caused you unhappiness.'

I laugh and admit he's right.

'Yes,' he continues, 'same for me, really. Intolerance and mockery all the way.' He gestures at his back.

'Oh,' I say, 'I'm sorry. It must have been horrible.'

Grost nods but grins at the same time. 'Absolutely horrible. But it made me who I am and I like to think that that, at least, means something good came out of it.'

And with that simple little spark of goodness he makes me love him all the more. 'Something good, indeed,' I agree. 'If mad on the subject of vampires.'

'Oh yes,' he agrees with mock earnestness. 'Quite mad.'

He drops the box with a dead toad in it into the hole he's dug and fills it in. We move on.

'What first interested you in them?' I ask. After all, he must have a pretty good reason – it's certainly never occurred to me to be obsessed with vampires.

'It was my father,' Grost says. 'When I was six or so I became suspicious of him. He rarely left the house and would often fly into the most terrible tempers. He had a smell to him, a sickly sweet odour that followed him around the house like a storm cloud. I was terrified of him but my sister was worse. She was a few years older than me, a beautiful girl whose natural happiness and humour I saw crushed slowly by my father's violence over the years. At night I would hear him creep into our room and one night I saw his face as it hovered over her, lit by the moon. There was a shadow of black around his mouth . . . blood! I was sure of it! I was convinced he was a vampire, feeding off my sister . . . Even my young mind realised that I had to act or she would face the consequences.'

'What did you do?' I ask.

'One night I lay in wait for him. I used the sheets and pillow to make it look like my bed was occupied and then I hid behind the door. I have never been good at standing for long periods – my spine burns like a blacksmith's poker after a while. Still I waited, knowing that if I lost my courage now I might never be able to act again. Eventually, I heard his footsteps on the floor - boards. He was a big man, heavy, and the wood creaked beneath him as if it found it as hard to bear him as we did.

'He came into the room and looked towards my bed. Satisfied that I was asleep, he walked slowly over to where my sister lay. She too pretended to sleep, his eyes tightly closed, her breathing heavy. I knew it was fake: I had lain awake listening to her often enough to know what she really sounded like when she was alseep. She just hoped it would keep him away. I often wonder if she knew what I had been planning, whether she was aware of me watching over her. Maybe . . .

'Father didn't care if she was sleeping or not. He had his appetite and his hunger had grown too strong to ignore. He drew closer, leaning over her bed, his huge broad back blocking out the faint white light from the window behind him.

'I ran at him, holding the sharpened wooden stake that I had spent the day preparing firmly in my hands. The wood had come from a broken chair-leg and my fingers were full of splinters. I was a clumsy child, determined yet gawky.

'I shoved the stake as hard into him as I could. Still, it was a terrible, lousy attempt. It is very hard to puncture someone's heart with a piece of wood using only the strength in your arms. Especially when you're just a weak child.

'It hurt him, though, and it hung from the wound in his back, bouncing up and down as he jumped around the room trying to reach for it.'

Grost stands there, a dead toad in one hand, an empty box in the other. Today's tasks are quite forgotten; his mind is lost in his own history.

'I was terrified,' he continues. 'I didn't know what to

do. Then I thought of the knife . . .'

He looks at his hand as if still expecting to see a weapon in it. Instead, he finds only a dead toad. He drops it in the box, buries it and we move on.

'It was the knife that I'd used to sharpen the stake,' he explains, 'and it was still hidden under my mattress.

'I watched my father bouncing around the room, trying to pull the stake from his back. I knew that if I didn't keep fighting then he would surely kill me, maybe even my sister too. She was sitting up in bed, looking from him to me, the fear on her face so strong that it almost broke my heart. I think that's what made me move in the end, that awful look of sheer dread on my lovely sister's face.

'I grabbed the knife and ran at the old man, swinging it at him, stabbing and slashing in a panic, only knowing that if I moved quickly enough he might not have a chance to fight back. If he had he would certainly have won. He could have picked me up and thrown me across the room with little effort.

'There was a lot of blood.'

Grost stops talking then and the look on his face tells me that he thinks he's said too much. Caught up in his own story, he has opened up more than he's comfortable with.

'It's all right,' I say, touching his arm, 'I understand.'

The look on his face is confused. He is partly grateful and partly angry: you can tell that he thinks understanding this moment from his childhood is something only he is capable of.

'He died,' he says simply, closing the door on the

memory. 'And I ran away from home that very night. I could hardly stay, after all.'

'But surely . . . if he was a vampire . . .'

Grost shakes his head. 'He wasn't a vampire – that was just a child's imagination doing its best to understand something that was beyond it. No,' he says, wistful again, 'he was perfectly human. But he was also the most terrible monster I've ever faced.'

He stoops down and begins digging. For a moment I think he's not going to talk any more, that he's scared himself into silence. I underestimate him, though: he is stronger than that.

'I wandered around, working for food and learning what I could about monsters. I met Kronos years later,' Grost says as he stands up from the small hole he has made. I fetch a box and drop a dead toad in it. It feels disgusting but I want to help. 'And in him I saw a man as broken by his own family as I was. I also saw a man who understood the nature of monsters, someone indeed who knew the most important thing of all.'

'And what's that?' I ask.

Grost smiles. 'He knew, my dear, that they must be fought!'

Eighteen

Father Volk Faces His Demons

There can be little doubt that we are living in an age without God. At what point He abandoned us I could not say but abandon us He most certainly has. One only has to look at the faces in my weekly congregation to find proof. Has any other heavenly envoy been faced with such an uphill climb of sin and perdition?

Clyde Lorrimer, his face the colour of yew berries, reeking of last night's ale and tobacco. He always sits at the back of the church, in the belief that I will not see him doze away during my sermon, preferring his dreams of full tankards to my offer of redemption.

Hollis won't be far away, either. He's the landlord of the White Hart and the source of most of my congregation's weaknesses. He thinks I don't know that he has a couple of doxies flipping customers in one of the inn's upstairs rooms. A village the size of ours and still we're awash with drunkards and whores.

Come forward a row and we find Morris Blake, footman to the Durwards (who have not graced my company for so long that I have washed my hands of their shabby souls). Morris would have no need to pay for his carnal sin – he is a handsome young man and knows it. Like all members of his trade, a more vain and polished creature cannot be imagined. Yet by all accounts – and yes, I mean the gossip that floods across the church step like the Red Sea itself, catching the impure up in its waves – he has no interest in the women of the village. Which makes him the strangest footman I ever heard of.

Then we come to the Gluckhavens, a mother and father as aged as Methuselah himself, leaning on one another for support while their son – born to Dorothy Gluckhaven at an age when one might think such things were quite beyond her – gazes across the pews and dreams of freedom. No chance of that with old Ernest Gluckhaven's cows to look after. They are a weighty beef millstone around that young lad's neck, for sure.

But where does Freddie Gluckhaven's gaze fall while he dreams? On the form of Sally Somerton, of course, though if her father ever caught him looking he'd likely smite him with all the wrath of God Himself. Somerton is a man of violence, arms as big as oak trunks that look uncomfortable crammed into his shirtsleeves, as if they were made to pound and punch rather than stay inactive. His temper is as well-known as the protective-ness he feels for his daughter. For Freddie Gluckhaven, even looking at Sally might get him in the same state as the dried-up cows his father raises for slaughter.

Here is Dr Marcus, a man who professes to believe in God and yet spends all his days thinking that he can second-guess His work. I have no time for physicians:

you can be sure that their arrogance will find them out when the Last Trump sounds.

Then the Sorrells: the angry son, the vacant father and the daughter who holds them all together. If they could but understand that God provides all the answers they need then perhaps they could get on and stop looking so miserable all the time. It's hard to preach the enriching scripture when faced with such damp clay.

Of course, today won't help as we gather to bury another of their number alongside what was left of young Petra Wilkins. Ah! Petra Wilkins! A fine-looking girl in her time, a real testament to the artistry of the Lord. I would often gaze down on her during prayers: she knelt on such a beautiful pair of knees and made prayer seem all the more beautiful when uttered through such full lips. She is naught but a sack of filth now. Praise the Lord.

The service is briefer than I might like but the families are so distracting, what with their sobbing and the intrusion of words of remembrance. If only they would understand that this is a religious ceremony, where we remember how God can strike us down on a whim if He so desires. It's not an excuse to waffle on about how lovely someone was – they've plenty of time for that unconstructive nonsense when they get home. Will I ever save their souls?

Finally, the graves are filled with dirt and I can escape the sunshine and the congregation's persistent sobbing. (The dead girls are in Heaven, for goodness' sake: why are you so upset?) The church is the only place to keep cool in these long days of summer and I often stroll along the nave, thinking on the miracle of God and giving my robes a good waft to encourage a blessed cooling updraught.

I listen to the villagers file away, back to their lives of sin and corruption, and am relieved to have them gone. It is clear to me that the one thing that really ruins the life of a church is its congregation. Things are so much better without them.

Through the window – a rather bland representation of St George at its centre, killing the dragon in a most lacklustre manner – I can see Dr Marcus talking to young Paul Durward. Had I not been thinking of that family earlier? I see he's placing a wreath at the base of his father's statue. Awful eyesore it is: how is a man to commune with God when he has that ugly thing looming over him? It is such a trial.

I gaze upon the shadow of the crucifix on the wall and take comfort from it. It reminds me that I'm not the only holy man who has had to suffer.

While I watch, the arms of the cross flex and bend and I'm struck dumb by the implications. Is my Lord to bestow upon me His gracious presence? Can He be stepping down from his place of execution – a representation of it, at least – in order to share in my suffering?

'My Lord?' I ask, turning away from the moving shadow to look towards what has cast it.

'If you wish,' comes the reply and there is a hot swipe across my cheek as its hand lashes out and the nails dig delicate furrows. It flashes through my head that I should offer this lunatic my other cheek but I decide that

that particular passage of the New Testament can be safely ignored for now.

I run towards the altar. My way out of the building is blocked.

'Dear God!' I call but there is no answer as I feel the creature's nails dig into the back of my skull like a crown of thorns. I reach out, hoping to snatch something and pull myself to safety. My hands grab a rope and I realise that I shall die listening to the sound of our stupid little church bell. How often have I said that we deserve something finer? This tin monstrosity should be hanging round a cow's neck . . .

It is my only modicum of relief, knowing that I will never have to listen to the noise of that wretched piece of metal again. The blood fills my ears and I die to a sound of pealing as if the bell were chiming underwater, like that of a vessel lost at sea.

Nineteen

Marcus Feels the Need to Pray

It is clear that Lady Durward will not condescend to meet me. I am saddened by her determination – a determination unsoftened by the passage of seven long years since her husband died in my care – but I accept it. Paul climbs inside the carriage and the footman, a handsome young man called Blake, lifts the steps and closes the door behind him. Sparing me a rather apologetic look, Blake taps the side of the coach and the driver urges the horses on as the footman hops onto the back. The vehicle moves away.

I have been snubbed. But no matter, there are far more important matters than the sensibilities of the local gentry to concern me at the moment.

As I'm walking back past the church, the bell begins to ring. Too late, Father, I think, your congregation has left, heartily sick of your waffle.

As I'm stepping through the lychgate I hear a cry from inside the building and I turn on my heels to see what the problem is. No doubt Volk has given himself rope-burn by tolling his silly little bell.

It is not a burn that has caused him to scream.

Volk is hanging from the bell rope like a pendulum, his always ruddy face now a disgusting purple, his tongue bloated like one of Grost's toads and hanging from between his lips. I run to help but it's clear that I'm too late even as I slip in the viscera that have spilled from a large gash cut across his torso.

For a moment I'm struck dumb by the sight of Volk, tied up and emptied like a bag of trash, his hollow body turned into a mockery of the bell that rings above him. Who – or what – could have done such a thing?

I run back to the door and shout for help. This is a business that I shouldn't conduct on my own.

'What is it, doctor?' asks Luke, running up from the graveyard where he has no doubt been taking a snooze under the shade of a tree. 'What's wrong?'

What's wrong? What's wrong is that you're going to have to dig a third hole today, after all . . .

'Father Volk,' I say. 'Someone's—'

Luke rushes past me and I hear his shout of alarm from behind me as he catches sight of the priest's swinging corpse. 'Fuck a cow sidewise,' he whispers in what will later occur to me as the most inappropriate last rites that Father Volk could have hoped for. 'How's he done that, then?'

'It can hardly be self-inflicted,' I say, 'Now help me cut him down.'

It takes Luke a few minutes to find something sharp enough to cut through the bell rope. He settles eventually on a short saw that he uses to keep the yew trees in the graveyard manageable.

I pull the altar across so that I can use it to climb up and cut the rope.

'That's blasphemy, isn't it?' Luke asks as I trample on the altar cloth.

'Leaving him hanging is worse,' I assure him. 'Do you really think God would begrudge me the assistance?'

Luke shrugs. His God is very much the same as the deceased Father Volk's, an unreasonable being that would put a lightning bolt through you as soon as blink.

Cutting the rope is hard work, not helped by Luke's whining as he tries to pull Volk's body down to keep the rope taut.

'I'm getting him all over me,' he bleats. As the rope finally parts and the corpse drops to the ground in a splatter of shed organs, he dashes behind a pew to be sick.

I can hardly blame him. It's a vile business and it's only due to my having a stomach that has long become inured to the horror of gore that I'm not joining him. Once you've seen enough of people's insides you begin to disassociate the flesh from the soul. You have to.

From my vantage point I can look down on the whole interior of the church and I see something that I was too distracted to notice earlier. There are tiny footprints, running from the shed blood that has pooled below where Volk was hanging. They don't lead to the vestibule (of course not, I realise, because I was running towards that and would have cut off the attacker's escape) but rather towards the rear of the church.

I jump down and squat over the flagstones to try and

identify the shape of the footprints. It's impossible to tell whether they might belong to a man or a woman – when you run you only leave prints from the balls of your feet, and they are no more than small circular dots.

I may not be able to identify them but I can certainly follow them.

Behind the altar is a small door leading to the vestry and I follow the footprints through it. There is another door that opens out into the rear of the churchyard.

There is no more sign of the footprints as I step outside – there was a lot of blood but not enough to track so far – but I run my hands through the bushes that line the rear fence. Some have clearly been forced apart as someone – probably not so big, judging by the limited damage – jumped from the fence, through the bushes and into the field beyond. I follow their example, snapping a few more branches of my own, and emerge, scratched and none the wiser, to look out across an empty field and the road beyond.

Whoever – whatever – did this is long gone.

'Doctor?' Luke is shouting. 'Doctor? Where are you?'

His voice is taking on a real edge of panic as he starts to think I've left him there with the body of his former employer and spiritual adviser.

'Coming!' I shout and climb back the way I came.

Twenty

Carla Has Little Interest in Her Lunch

After a long morning of burying dead toads you fixate on lunch. You might think that such a duty would lower anyone's appetite but familiarity makes a comedy out of anything and by the time Grost and I had finished marking one side of the forest we were tossing the creatures to each other with no squeamishness whatsoever. Though even Grost was a bit disgusted by the one that exploded across the brim of his stovepipe hat. We decided that it must have gone off in the heat, making it more explosive than the others.

We arrive back at Marcus's house to find Kronos, bare-chested, sitting cross-legged on the roof (meditating, according to Grost – showing off, according to me) with Marcus's handyman, Clyde Lorrimer watching him as if he were the devil himself.

'No need for it,' Lorrimer says when he spots us. 'A man can sit wherever he likes but he's asking for trouble up there, isn't he?'

'He likes the sense of perspective,' Grost explains.

'And looking down on people,' I add.

'That I can believe,' says Lorrimer, offering me a

smile that makes me think of the exploding toad. Its guts were certainly a similar colour to his teeth.

'If there's anything I can do for you, milady,' he says, 'you will ask, won't you?'

It's obvious that Clyde Lorrimer has designs on me and I decide that now's as good a time as any to nip matters in the bud.

'Clyde,' I say, 'do you know what happened to the last man who lifted my skirts?'

A look of what can only be described as euphoria crosses his face as he considers this. 'No, Miss Carla,' he says, 'but I'm hoping you'll tell me.'

'Indeed I will,' I say. 'He lost his ear.'

'Lost his ear?' asks Clyde.

'Lost his ear,' I repeat. 'But then, I spat it so far into the undergrowth that he didn't have a chance of finding it, really.'

Clyde's face grows rather pale at this thought. 'Oh,' he says. 'There's no need for that.'

Grost is chuckling as we go inside and see what we can find to eat.

We're cutting up bread, cheese and pickles when Marcus walks in.

'Kronos is on the roof,' he says.

'We know,' Grost replies. 'He'll come down when he's ready.'

'I hope you don't mind,' I say, pointing at the food, 'but we've worked up an appetite.'

'Help yourself,' says Marcus, 'though you'll have to forgive me if I don't join you. I can't quite stomach the idea of food at the moment.'

'Why?' I ask, taking a bite of some cheese.

He tells us, and I decided that maybe I can't stomach the idea of food now either.

A pair of legs suddenly appears on the other side of the window as Kronos climbs down the outside of the house.

'Is it time for lunch?' he asks as he steps inside.

'Listen to what Marcus has to tell you first,' I suggest. 'You might save yourself the effort.'

Kronos's stomach is clearly made of stronger stuff than mine. He works his way unconcernedly through the bread and pickles while Marcus repeats his story.

'Fascinating,' he says, his mouth full of bread.

'Not the word I'd use,' Marcus replies, irritated at his friend's conduct.

Kronos swallows. 'We are pursuing a vampire that feeds by draining the life force of its victim, yes?'

'Yes,' I say.

'Then why is the local priest torn open and left to hang? If it was the vampire, why would it waste the opportunity to feed?'

'Vampires never do that,' says Grost. 'Like all carnivores, they're too driven by their sense of self-preservation. If it was going to kill him it should have done so in the same manner as before.'

'Perhaps it really hated him?' I suggest.

'He was easy to hate,' says Marcus.

Grost shakes his head. 'Kronos is right. It doesn't make the least bit of sense.'

'Unless?' asks Kronos, looking at Grost.

Grost looks back at his friend for a moment and then

his face becomes grim. 'That's highly unlikely, surely?'

'What?' asks Marcus.

Grost sighs, removes his spectacles and begins to polish them. Anything, it seems, rather than speak his thoughts aloud.

'Unless?' asks Kronos again.

'Unless,' snaps Grost impatiently, 'we're dealing with more than one vampire.'

Twenty-One

What the Beer Brought Out of Luke Hopkins

Hanging there he were, like a pig on a gibbet, with me ankle-deep in guts. And the doctor weren't no help, he were far too busy climbing over the furniture and buggering off for a walk in the graveyard. Couldn't take it, see, he were sick to his stomach, he were, chucking up all over the floor.

He were and all, Clyde Lorrimer, I don't care what you say about him, he ain't got the guts for that sort of thing and I knows it as a fact as I've seen it with me own two eyes. He was worse than a girl. Moaning and spewing, spewing and moaning. It's only thanks to me that we got poor Father Volk down in the end.

I used my little saw, see, the one I uses to keep the trees trim. Cut him down I did, and rolled him up in one of those what-do-you-call-'ems . . . you know, the big cloth they have on the altar. All embroidered with crosses and that. Gold braid. You know . . . the cloth for a bloomin' altar. What do they call 'em? Eh?

Altar cloth, that's the feller.

So we wrapped him up in one of those and that was a job in itself, so many bits were lying all over the place.

You can pull a face, Bob, but I'm just telling it like it was. There were kidneys, livers and lights, everywhere you looked. Who would've knowed a human body had so much offal in it? I had to work my way up and down the front of the church to make sure we'd caught it all. Can't have one of the ladies coming in and going for a tumble by slipping on a bit of lung, now, can you?

Anyway, that's how I found it! I reckon as Father Volk had snatched at the feller who was killing him and pulled it loose. Well, you would, wouldn't you? If some bastard was doing you in and you're wearing your guts for stockings you'd fight back, surely? Stands to reason.

There you go, take a look at that. Beautiful, ain't it? Yanked it right off the bastard's coat I reckon.

Eh? Whose coat? Don't be dense, Bill, how many coats have gold buttons on 'em like this 'un? It's a soldier's coat, ain't it? And who do we know that's turned up recently wearing one of those?

Twenty-Two

Marcus Admires His Handiwork

Later, I sit down with Kronos. Carla and Grost are still in the forest, burying toads and leaving behind them a trail of tied ribbons to mark where the boxes are buried. I dare say it's useful work. Yes, probably very useful indeed. Probably.

'You think I should be out there, don't you?' says Kronos, rolling one of those foul-smelling smokesticks of his. 'Running around the countryside and hiding in graveyards?'

'I certainly think you should be doing something,' I admit, 'especially if it stops you filling my house with the smell of those awful things.'

'It's a Chinese herb,' Kronos says, with a smile.

'Chinese herb indeed,' I reply, with a heavy note of sarcasm in my voice. 'You never used to smoke it.'

'I never used to need it,' he says. 'It calms me – these days that is a difficult job.'

I accept that his lifestyle is somewhat more unpleasant than that of most people. We sit in silence for a while.

'The problem,' he says after a moment, 'is hunting a

creature of intelligence. When you're tracking an animal you have an advantage in that it doesn't know you're on its tail, and even if it does it will only ever act like that particular animal acts: it is constrained by its nature. A vampire has all the ingenuity and cunning of its hunter.'

'Even if you do say so yourself!'

Kronos smiles. 'Even if I do. So the only way to capture it is for it to make sufficient mistakes or to be sufficiently unsubtle in its movements.'

'All the while knowing that with every day that passes another victim may die.'

'The more people who die the easier it gets. That's the really difficult part of the business.'

I can see the logic of this but am still not altogether satisfied. 'But still, how can you learn anything if you stay sitting here?'

Kronos takes another draw on his smokestick. 'The only time I can be of any use outside is if I am lucky enough to be in the vicinity when the creature actually strikes. To be on the ground when the trail is hot – then you are in active pursuit, both of you running through the night! There is a chance then: it all comes down to speed. Outside of that, though, the only tracking I can do is in my head. I can make deductions based on evidence. To do that I don't even need to open my eyes, let alone leave the house.'

'Very well. So we can narrow down the vampire's identity by using logical deduction, I can see that. Well, it feeds on youth, desperate to prolong its existence. So we're looking for someone old . . .'

'Quite the reverse. It is a creature rich with the energy

of youth, so we are looking for someone with a rosiness to their cheeks!'

'Oh, right . . .' Again, I can follow this line of reasoning, though it doesn't narrow the field much. 'So what else do we know?'

'Is there anyone who is newly arrived in the area?'

I thought for a while. 'No, I don't think so . . . Oh, wait, there are three visitors at the White Hart. They claim to be ex-soldiers – a rough lot, to be sure.'

'Very well, they may be worth investigating. However, if we exclude them there is something else that is rather suggestive. If the vampire is in fact one of the locals then circumstances have demanded that it escalate its feeding. I would have thought it could easily take a little of someone's life energy but not so much as we have seen with Ann and Petra. An attack like that is bold, brazen. It works everyone up, makes them frightened. To continue such a feeding habit would very swiftly bring the light of attention to bear on the creature in question. So why the sudden need to feed so deeply?'

'I couldn't begin to guess.'

'No,' Kronos agrees. 'For the moment, neither can I. But it is important, I think.'

'What about the attack in the church? Do you really think that that was the work of someone – or something – else entirely?'

Kronos nods. 'A vampire does not waste food. The priest was slaughtered viciously, his life force squandered. Why? And such an act of barbarism . . . the style is completely different. Your problem has doubled, I'm sure of it.'

'Wonderful. So we hope the toads do the trick, then, eh?'

'The toads will confirm what we already know: that you have a vampire in the area.'

'Hardly seems worth the effort.'

'They also do something else, something far more valuable. They show that we are onto the creature, that we know what it is and that we are actively pursuing it. Hopefully that will make the vampire nervous. Nervousness breeds mistakes. Remember?'

I look at him and smile.

'Of course I remember.'

It was in the early days of the Ireland campaign and most of us were still green and homesick enough to be on edge over there. We had taken Drogheda and Wexford and were marching north.

On hearing reports of Royalist supporters massing in a small town near Lisburn, our regiment was detached from the main fighting force in order to investigate.

Rather than go marching straight into a town that could have been filled with Catholic Irish and the visiting Royalist Scots our commander, a sinewy lump of scar tissue and chewing tobacco by the name of Saunders, led us around the periphery of the town. He had decided that a little covert surveillance would be the best way to proceed.

All seemed quiet enough until we came upon a sizeable shack hidden away in the woodland to the north of the town. The shack was guarded by a bored-looking fellow who was silenced with such speed that he probably didn't know his throat had been cut until his pipe got too difficult to smoke.

'What have we got 'ere?' Saunders wondered, opening the shack's doors and finding himself face to face with a gunpowder store the size of a small house. 'Bugger me' was his informed military opinion.

It was soon decided that we would take as much of the gunpowder with us as we could carry and blow up the rest. After all, it made no sense to leave such valuable munitions in the hands of the enemy. We had a barrel each strapped to our backs and a young lad called Piper was charged with running a trail of gun-powder away from the store to act as a fuse so we could buy ourselves time to run for cover before the whole thing went sky-high.

Piper was not confident in the execution of his duty. Despite constant reassurance that the gunpowder could not simply ignite of its own accord, he was sweating in panic as he slowly walked backwards through the undergrowth with a tipped-up keg in his hands.

'I didn't sign up for this,' he kept saying. 'This stuff just ain't natural. A sword, that's a proper weapon – this stuff's just grains of hell.'

'Oh, stop your moaning,' said Kronos in the end, tired of watching Piper's slow work. 'Let me do it.'

He moved to take the keg from Piper when a rustling in the trees caused the younger man to flinch. 'Who's that?' he cried, twisting to look. He stared up into the greenery, shaking with fear, only to see a squirrel dart from one branch to another.

'A Royalist tree rat,' said Kronos. 'Now get on with it before someone does turn up.'

Once he'd finished laying the trail of powder, Piper struck a light with some irritation and promptly learned that, while looking around in panic, he had clumsily filled the tops of his boots with gunpowder. He discovered this after a spark from his tinderbox landed there and blew him, and the barrel of gunpowder on his back, heavenwards.

Kronos, only a few feet away at the time, was sent hurtling through the air, his face and hair singed and several blackened pieces of Piper peppering the front of his uniform. Worse still, a flying shard of Piper's sword cut a line right across his belly, opening a deep wound. In fact, the only good news for poor Kronos was that his body shielded the keg of gunpowder on his back from the blast and thus saved him from going up himself.

The explosion did ignite the trail of gunpowder, however, so we had to run for cover, dragging Kronos along the ground behind us, his hands pressed hard against his belly in order to keep his guts in.

We were not so clandestine any more, either, though we were lucky that the explosion of the gunpowder store and the subsequent chaos more than covered our escape. The building took to the sky like a soaring phoenix, the noise enough to deafen us for some time after.

'Nearly dead because of a bloody squirrel,' says Kronos, running his finger along the scar on his belly.

I lean forward and admire my handiwork. 'Lucky you had me there, really,' I say.

'Look,' I add. 'Sorry if I get impatient but you must remember that these villagers are my people. I know them well and each death hits all the harder. But you know what you're doing, and as long as you're not avoiding the confrontation . . .' I point at his scar. 'I could never doubt your bravery. I know you have guts – after all, I've seen them!'

'Indeed you have.' Kronos pats me on the shoulder. 'We will find this creature soon, my friend. Don't worry, it will stick its neck out too far and before you know it . . .' He claps his hands. 'We will be there to cut it off.'

Twenty-Three

Carla Loves to Dance

Isn't wine wonderful? I mean, really, it's like the most brilliant thing ever and ever and ever and . . . isn't it? Not only does it stop you being thirsty but it also helps you to be really good at things. It makes you much funnier than you are normally. It makes you sing better and as for your dancing . . . well, you're pretty much unstoppable.

I think it was because of the toads. And the dead priest. And the vampires. And everything. But I really, really wanted some wine this evening, just to take my mind off it, you know? To put a smile back on my, back on my . . . on my . . .

Marcus has lots of lovely wine. He must like it nearly as much as I do. He showed me where he kept it (which was a bit of a mistake, to be honest, but I'm glad he did) and I sat down and had a look through the bottles, just to see which one I liked the look of best.

Not that I haven't drunk wine before, of course. Oh yes. Lots of it. But most of it was poured out of a jug by George Barrow, the landlord of the . . . erm . . . the . . .

whatever it was called . . . Toad and Hunchback, the Kronos Codpiece . . . erm . . . something.

Anyway, the point is that I didn't know which sort of wine I liked and having been given a choice I decided the best thing was probably just to try a bit of each. Just a little bit. Well, enough to get the taste, you know. A few cupfuls.

So, I'm singing about the Bad Old Bishop of Bath and Wells and trying to make a nice hat out of a table I'd found when they all start talking about the bloody dead priest again, like we haven't heard enough about that already.

So I got a bit cross. Which isn't like me. No, really. I'm a very . . . a very . . . not – cross sort of girl. Anyway, I did, and there may have been shouting, I can't honestly remember, I was a little bit, what-do-you-call-it . . . when you've had too much wine . . . that, I was. Very much.

I decided to go to the stables and leave them to it. At least in there I could just get on with enjoying my evening, maybe sing a few more songs, maybe dance for a while. You know. Whatever I wanted.

The having-too-much-wine thing was starting to wear off by the time Kronos appeared, which is just as well because otherwise I wouldn't have been able to be quiet about his stupid frowny face. He never bloody smiles, that one, it's always grumpy-got-to-fight-vampires with him. Which would be fine if he ever actually left the house and found one. Since he doesn't I don't quite see the point in his taking it all so seriously. He should enjoy himself a bit more, don't you think?

I tell him this, maybe a few times, can't remember. And, give him his due, he does smile in the end. Though that might be because I'd taken my clothes off, which sometimes happens with wine, I find. He must have had a few drinks too because his clothes ended up coming off as well. For quite a while. Which cheered me up, I must say: he's one of those men who look much nicer without clothes on than they do with them. Though I imagine it's hard to hunt vampires when you're naked. Well, not hard. I mean . . . Oh . . . Oh God . . . I do feel a bit unwell. Maybe there was something wrong with the . . . you know, red stuff, nice to drink . . .

God.

This is going to be so embarrassing in the morning . . .

Twenty-Four

Freddie Gluckhaven's Heart Breaks

'Of course, mother,' I insist, 'the cows couldn't be happier – I'd hardly leave them be otherwise.'

I swear the old bird thinks the beasts will expire if they're not under constant supervision. She sits on the porch, rocking back and forth on that damn creaky chair of hers and never lets her eye off the field. Wouldn't be so bad but every passing whim falls to me to fulfil. Is it any wonder that father can barely move a few steps these days? She wore him to a standstill! Now she's moved on to me, whittling me down like a wooden peg. If it weren't for Sally I'd probably go quite mad.

My Sally. The most wonderful, bright, beautiful girl in the world.

If it weren't for her blasted father she'd be perfect!

No. I won't impose her father's failings on her, any more than she holds mother against me. You can't choose your parents and that's a fact.

'I won't be long,' I promise – though, God help me, I'll be as long as I think I can get away with: it's only these occasional hours with Sally that make life worth living.

I cut into the forest, only too aware that mother will

be watching me all the way, keeping those narrowed little eyes focused on my back until the trees get in the way and finally I can relax. It's as if the entire burden of the farm has been lifted from me. I'm almost light-headed with relief as I run through the trees. One day, I know, I'm going to keep running and never go back. I just won't be able to help myself.

Of course, I won't be running alone.

Sally jumps out from behind a tree, grabbing my back and then wrapping her arms around my neck.

'There's monsters in the forest, young Freddie,' she growls. 'Haven't you heard?'

Laughing, I drop to my knees and fling her down in front of me.

'You just found one, my love!' I tell her, nuzzling her neck and roaring softly.

She squeals as I gently bite her smooth flesh and wrestle with her. Then she slips away and runs off into the trees.

'All right,' I say. 'That's how you want to play, is it?'

I give chase. It's not difficult – she's laughing so much that even if I lose sight of her among the dark tree trunks all I'll have to do is follow the evidence of my ears.

The light flickers through the trees as I run and I have the strange sensation that I'm dreaming my journey beneath the canopy of leaves and branches. Time seems to slow with every pulse of sunshine, as if the world is becoming nothing but a series of still moments that I'm passing through.

Sally laughs again and that just adds to my feeling of being separate from the real world. I could be home in bed, dreaming of escape. Or daydreaming as I squeeze milk from the teats of those damned cows. Or sitting on the porch, listening to mother rage against a world that just won't do what she wants it to.

I stop running for a moment and press my hands to my temples. I feel as though a mask has settled over my head, something that is in between me and the real world. I want to scratch it away but there's nothing there.

I catch my breath for a moment, rub my face and brush away the mood that has settled over me. I'm just tired, I think, and sick of the day-to-day chores and the prison that is my life. None of which are good enough reasons to spoil the few moments I have now. That little bit of time with the woman I love most in the whole world.

That time will be short.

Sally's got a head start now and I have to run fast and hard. The forest is filled with run-off trenches where the water from the hills drains away in the winter. They're all dry now, and I leap them rather than climb down and then back up.

My mood turns like a tossed coin and I'm laughing myself as I sail through the air, struggling to keep my footing in the slippery undergrowth. Even here, in the shade, the day is hot and I've got a sweat on by the time Sally's in sight.

She's looking worried – she thinks something's hap - pened to me. She looks around and around, unnerved to suddenly find herself alone. Maybe she's thinking about what happened to Petra and Ann, or about poor old

Volk strung up in his own church. Maybe she's wishing she had never come running in here after all.

I sneak up as quietly as I can, half of me loving the game, the other half thinking it's time I grew up. To hell with it, I tell that older, more sensible part of me, there'll be plenty more hours of grown-up misery today. Enjoy the childishness while you can.

I leap on Sally, laughing as she screams, my hands diving under her skirts in devilish hunger for something sweet to explore.

'Freddie!' she shouts, punching me on the arm. 'I thought you'd gone . . .'

'I'm not going anywhere,' I tell her and stop the rest of her complaints with my mouth. She doesn't seem to mind.

Later, we lie hot and tired at the foot of an oak so tall that it cannot help but make you feel small and fragile.

'I've got to get back,' Sally says, 'before father starts wondering where I am.'

I sigh and pick at the bark of the tree. 'One day,' I say, 'we're going to stop doing what they tell us. We're going to say to hell with the lot of them and be happy.'

Sally looks up at me and her eyes show that she doesn't believe herself when she says: 'One day.'

She's so damn scared of her old man and I can't say I blame her – he scares *me* a fair bit! Still, I refuse to live my whole life around what parents say. There comes a time when you have to stand on your own two feet and if she finds that hard then I'll just have to help her.

She smiles but there's no hope in her expression whatsoever. It makes me sad.

'I'll walk back with you,' I say.

A flash of fear passes over her face. 'Don't be mad,' she says. 'You can't come up to the house.'

'Just to the edge of the forest,' I say. 'Then I'll know you'll be safe.'

Sally smiles again. 'Don't be silly, there's nothing here to be scared of.'

'Tell that to the Sorrells.'

She doesn't argue any more.

We get to our feet and, hand in hand, begin to walk towards Sally's home. The air around us is filled with the scents of the woodland, and with the oppressive air of things unsaid. How the love between us was never choked dead by the weight of others' opinions I'll never know.

'I can manage from here,' she says, letting go of my hand and reaching up to kiss my cheek. 'You don't have to go all the way.'

'I'll watch,' I say, 'so I know you're all right.'

Sally shakes her head but she's smiling. 'Such an old woman,' she says. 'I'm capable of looking after myself, you know.'

'I know,' I say, 'but I also enjoy watching you walk.' I squeeze her hand and let her go.

She hesitates for a moment and later I'll wonder about that: what if she had waited a little longer? What if she had taken just one more kiss?

Sally walks ahead and approaches one of the run-off trenches. Carefully, dropping a hand to the ground to steady herself, she descends out of sight. A few seconds later she reappears, stumbling slightly as she climbs out of the trench. She giggles with embarrassment and checks over her shoulder to see if I noticed. I smile and blow her a kiss.

Somewhat ruefully, she returns it and continues on her way.

I lean back against the trunk of one of the trees and watch again as she goes down into another trench.

That was the point, I will think later. That was the point at which I last saw her and she still had a chance of survival. Not that anything could have been done: however much I may always be haunted by that moment I will never be so blind as to believe that. She was struck so quickly – a moment of terror as her scream echoes through the trees . . .

'Sally!' I shout, already on the move.

Ahead of me I see her reappear, hands waving in the air, fighting to hold onto something that will steady her as she rises back up from below.

'Sally?'

She turns and, in that brief moment as the sunlight lands on the face of an old woman, I am reminded of that feeling of dislocation from earlier. That unsettling belief that I was not in the real world at all but rather some terrible, loose, dreamy version of it.

She falls, her aged legs not strong enough to hold her up.

I reach her in time to feel her last breath on my face. There is nothing else, no final words, no explanation, just that fragile puff of warm, damp air.

And with that the best thing in my life – the only good thing, in fact – is gone.

Twenty-Five

Brothers in Blood – The Memoirs of Professor Herbert Grost: Volume One (Unpublished)

I heard the man scream. A terrible noise, raw and filled with the most chilling sense of pain.

I had been sitting in the sunshine, considering the many varied ways in which the vampire reflects the darkness in all of us. (Is there any more global thirst than the thirst for youth?) My breakfast was sitting heavily in my belly but it had gone some small way towards dealing with the effects of the wine we'd drunk the night before.

I'm not very good at drinking. It tends to make me talk a lot. Which, given that I have a habit of going on anyway, can be positively lethal in polite company. Especially when you consider that my main subject of conversation revolves around monstrous bloodsucking creatures. Honestly, I really can kill a dinner party stone dead.

Add to that the fact that it tends to give me a terrible headache the next day and you will understand why I approach wine with caution. Last night it had crept up on me rather, sneaked in from the side when I wasn't looking. My head was displeased with my lack of internal security.

On hearing the scream, Kronos burst from the stables, sword in his hand.

'Grost?' he shouted.

'Here,' I replied. 'I heard it.'

Carla appeared in the doorway behind him, tugging her skirt straight and looking ever so slightly green.

'Someone needs help,' Kronos said and moved to push past me.

I grabbed his arm. 'That was not the sound of a man who needs help,' I replied. 'It was the sound of a man for whom help would be too late. Now go and get dressed. You can't run about the forest naked – you'll disturb the squirrels.'

Kronos glanced down, realising for the first time that he was utterly without clothes. He looked confused for a moment. Then he nodded.

'Thank you, my friend,' he said and ran back into the stable to get dressed.

'Spoilsport,' said Carla. She brushed past me on her way the sit under the water pump for a while.

Dr Marcus came running out of the house.

'What was that?' he asked.

'Nothing good,' I replied honestly. 'Come with us and find out.'

Once Kronos was dressed, we took the horses into the forest. Carla stayed behind: she was clearly under the weather and I could hardly see the advantage in forcing her to join us.

We had little difficulty finding the unfortunate

Freddie Gluckhaven. The sound of his sobbing drew us to where he sat, the dead body of an old – or, at least, old *now* – woman in his arms.

'Dead,' he said. 'She's dead.'

Gluckhaven simply wouldn't hear of us examining the woman. He shook his head and held the body tighter and tighter. At one point there was the terrible sound of bones snapping beneath the strength of his grip. Thankfully he seemed deaf to it. It was the appearance of another person that finally made him let go.

'Sally?' said the older man as he walked towards us. 'That's not my Sally, is it?' He was a big man, arms thick with muscle and face red and veined from ale. He was not a man I would wish to pick a fight with, and I've fought with the best in my time.

'Sally Somerton,' said Marcus, only now realising whose body we were fretting over. 'Careful – that's her father. He has a temper.'

'Sally,' the man said again, his ruddy face quivering as he began to suspect the worst.

'Wait a minute, Ted,' said Marcus. 'We don't know who it is yet.'

'You think I don't know my own daughter?' he roared. 'And the little rat that's holding her?'

'Not now,' said Gluckhaven, letting go of her so that her father could see. 'She wouldn't want that.'

'Fuck yourself,' Somerton said. He pushed the boy out of the way so hard that Freddie lost his footing and hit the ground in a shower of earth and leaves. I noticed the look of sheer rage that appeared on the young man's face but also the fact that he immediately suppressed his anger. And not through fear of the lumbering giant in front of us, I thought, rather out of respect for the woman he had clearly loved. It was at that moment that I decided I had the utmost respect for young Freddie Gluckhaven. I could not honestly say the same for the poor girl's father.

'What did he do?' the man was asking. 'What did that little rat do, eh?'

'The blame doesn't lie with Freddie,' said Marcus, stepping between the two of them, as aware as I that real trouble could erupt if we didn't play this carefully. 'Would you let me look at her, please?'

Ted Somerton looked up at Marcus as if confused about who he was. Then a fragment of understanding crept into his expression and he nodded and stepped back. He and the young man stared at one another as Marcus bent to look at the body.

'Exactly the same as before,' he said. 'Not that we expected anything else.'

'Same as the Sorrell girl?' Somerton asked, not taking his stare off Gluckhaven. 'What is it, then? Plague?'

'We don't know what it is,' said Kronos before Marcus could reply – not that I believe for one moment that he would have started talking about vampires in front of these two.

'And who would you be?' Somerton asked. 'There's a good deal of talk about you, with your funny accent.' He looked at me and sneered, his face twisted with all the disgust of a man who had just caught a dog emptying its bowels in his house. 'And your weird friend,' he continued. He puffed out his chest, obviously determined to claw back some control over this situation. 'You has to wonder,' he continued, 'about the appearance of strangers at the same time as something like this happening, don't you?'

'Not really,' Kronos replied. 'I am an old friend of Dr Marcus and he contacted me for my advice on the matter.'

'Advice, is it?' said Somerton. 'And what advice have you to give?'

Kronos stared at him in silence for a moment and then replied. 'I advise you to take your daughter away and have her remains buried with the respect she deserves. Then let me get on with solving this mystery for you before someone else's daughter ends up dead.'

Somerton looked about to argue but Freddie Gluckhaven interrupted.

'Please don't,' he said. 'Not with her lying there – she's worth more than some stupid quarrel. Take her home. Love her. Let these people do whatever it is they can do.'

Somerton opened his mouth for a moment but then closed it. He bent down to pick up his daughter's body and walked off with it in his arms without saying another word.

Once he had gone, Gluckhaven walked over to us. He looked at Kronos. 'You mean what you say?' he asked. 'You can help find whatever did this?'

Kronos nodded.

Gluckhaven thought for a moment. 'Then I'll help you in any way I can. I loved Sally so very much . . .'

Marcus put a hand on the young man's arm. 'Tell us what happened.'

Gluckhaven shrugged. 'I saw nothing. She was walking home, I was watching her, she dropped out of sight in one of the drainage gullies and when she reappeared she was like this. By the time I got to her she was dead.'

Kronos looked over to the gully. 'It happened down there?' he asked.

Gluckhaven nodded. 'I suppose it must have done,' he said. 'There was nothing wrong with her before.'

Kronos walked over and jumped down into the deep trench. He looked over to me and nodded. 'Come on,' he said. 'Let us hunt.'

I do wish, when Kronos is in his hunter/tracker moods, that he would remember I find it hard to match his pace. He ran as fast as he could, his boots kicking up a flurry of leaves as he followed the signs of someone having travelled this route. I did my best to keep up, keeping one hand on my hat as I ran in his wake.

I'm not a bad tracker myself (all it takes is an observant eye, after all, and I have two of those) but the speed with which Kronos identifies a trail and then sticks to it is more like that of a dog than a human. He barely pauses, his eyes tracking the route almost too quickly for his feet to keep up.

After a few minutes we climbed out of the gully and dashed between the trees.

Kronos stopped and I came to a juddering halt behind him, only too relieved to be able to draw breath.

'The toads,' he said.

I looked around and realised that, yes, we were about to cross the line we had drawn through the boundary of the woodland. Close by I spotted a small twist of ribbon tied to the branch of an evergreen bush. That was how I had marked the location of the boxes. Kronos followed my gaze, strolled over, withdrew his sword and stabbed into the soil with it. He cut a wide circle, the freshly turned earth parting easily enough before he dug out the small wooden box. He threw it to me and I pulled back the lid. A fat toad jumped to freedom and I smiled.

'Well,' I said, 'guess what walked this way recently.'

'Did you doubt it?' Kronos asked.

'Not really,' I had to admit, 'but it's good to know for sure.'

Kronos walked a few more paces and then sunk to the ground once more. 'Coach tracks,' he said, looking ahead through the trees. 'We need to fetch the horses.'

Twenty-Six

Morris Blake Hires a Killer

Dearest Nell,

Soon our time will come! I have, today, completed a favour for the Durward household and have no doubt that its appreciation will be both considerable and swift.

I confess that I was a little concerned about the details of my mission to begin with. It seemed a dark business and not one I should readily involve myself in. Still, having thought about it – and yes, I'll admit it, having considered how it may improve my standing and therefore bring us closer together – I decided there was little sin in it. You remember I told you about the strangers recently arrived? The foreigner who dresses like a soldier, and his malformed assistant? Well, it cannot be said that their presence has been welcomed. They go about strange business in the forest and the foreigner has even threatened some of the local folk. Yesterday the local priest, Father Volk, was found murdered in his church. Murdered in such a terrible manner that I cannot begin to describe it to you. There was one clue as to who may have done such a thing: a button of the sort that might be found on a military uniform. It is a suggestive find, I'm sure you'll agree.

I have become convinced, along with others here, that these strangers need to be dealt with. They are a menace and they need to be removed from our company.

For some time a gentleman of distinction has been staying close by, a lauded veteran of the recent conflicts, now retired from combat in order to pursue a quieter existence. Mackendrick Kerro is his name, and I was asked if I might hire his services in order to encourage the strangers to depart the area. Of course, I was pleased to be able to make the gentleman's acquaintance and so I set out to meet him.

He is staying at our inn, the White Hart. Not that I want to give the impression he couldn't have had a finer roof over his head – I am sure he could – but I believe the simple establishment afforded him the privacy he desired.

Did you ever think I would be moving in such elevated circles, dearest?

I was made most welcome by Mr Kerro and a number of his select associates who were also travelling with him. I explained our problem to him and he was only too happy to help.

'Young man,' he said, 'I will not stand for ill behaviour from anyone, most certainly not a man besmirching the army's name by masquerading as one of its number.'

He told me a number of stories concerning his exploits during the campaign. You would have been proud to have seen me in such company!

I left him with the assurance that his assistance was deeply appreciated and returned to Durward Hall where I was able to pass on the news of a job well done.

Just you wait and see: everything's going to work out very well for us, I have no doubt!

Yours,

Morris

Twenty-Seven

Kerro Fights the Ale Regiment

I swear, should I ever catch sight of that doxy again I'll cut her from her flapping mouth to the canker-encrusted wound she infected me with. A man should not wake up with balls burning like coals. I could mull wine with them, they're so hot. Filthy bitch, and not worth the couple of coins I graced her with. You'd think a fellow who's fought in more wars than most men have had birthdays would be able to get a bit of quality cunt, wouldn't you? He certainly shouldn't have to pay for it only to end up rotting his bloody prick off.

Kerro, my lad, it's a fucking disgrace.

It would help if I could keep my thirst for booze down, of course. I woke up this morning with what felt like an entire fucking regiment marching through my skull. An ale regiment! Barley soldiers galloping on hop horses. My head's pounding so much that I can't even get to my feet for a few minutes. I just have to lie there, pipe in one hand, balls in the other, waiting for the pounding to quieten down enough for me to meet my fellow guests here at the White Hart without feeling the need to slice their heads off with my sword.

Of course, you might say that if I got up before lunchtime I'd have a better chance of finding the place quiet. You might say that. But then I'd have to punch your fucking teeth in for being so sanctimonious.

Eventually I manage to get upright, pull on my britches over that rank and treacherous organ and head downstairs. Grafton and Underhill are already in place, tankards in hand. This is good: it saves me having to put my hand in my pocket, I wouldn't want to have to exert myself that much at this tender hour of the afternoon.

'Well done, gents,' I say, helping myself to a their ale. 'You've organised breakfast.'

I can tell Grafton's not pleased – he sneers a little before offering his polite laugh. Difficult, that. If he didn't care about my helping myself to his drink I'd think he had no balls at all, but if he ever looks like caring too much I'll cut off the ones he does own. The chain of command is a fine line, that's for sure. A real fucking art.

The place is pretty quiet. You'd think our presence would guarantee Hollis a bit of decent trade – people wanting to rub shoulders with the war heroes, so to speak. Maybe they have Royalist leanings hereabouts, but it actually seems to keep them away.

A fat man's filling up one of the centre tables. I don't recognise him. He must be a traveller, though I pity the poor horse that has to carry his weighty arse.

There's also a dandified boy in a cape, some perfumed servant with ideas above his station. He stares at me as I come down the stairs. Never seen a real man in his life I suspect, probably all overcome with excitement.

I drain Grafton's beer, just to teach him a lesson, and stare at the fat man for a while. He's eating bread and cheese, filling that fat moon face of his. It makes me hungry, to my considerable surprise.

'When did we last eat anything?' I wonder aloud.

'We had that pie yesterday,' says Underhill. 'Tasted of dog.'

That strikes me as funny and I can't help but laugh. 'Trust you to know what dog tastes like, you fucking animal,' I tell him.

I sit down at the fat man's table.

'Yes?' he asks, mouth full of bread.

'Kerro,' shouts Hollis, 'please . . .'

Please . . . *Please* don't cause trouble, *please* don't get me in trouble, *please* don't kill anyone . . . Would that I should never have to tolerate the word 'please'. The ale army steps up its clamour a notch in my head and for a moment I have to close my eyes against the noise. I wish they'd quieten down for a bit.

'Shut up,' I shout. 'You're damned lucky to have us as your guests. You should be bending over backwards to keep us happy.'

'Or bending over forwards in Underhill's case,' says Grafton, laughing.

'Piss off,' Underhill says. But he's used to the joke and doesn't really rise to it. Underhill's good like that, he has an even temper. Not me. I'm always going off on a rage. Blame the ale army – it's their drums I march to.

'I think you've had enough of that,' I tell the fat man. 'If you eat any more you're likely to burst and then we'll be wading through your guts for the rest of the day.'

'Please, Kerro,' says Hollis, *again*. 'If you want food I'll make you food – it's no problem.'

'I don't want you to make me food,' I say. 'I have food here.' I reach over and help myself to a piece of cheese. It's not bad: strong and tasty.

'Look,' says the fat man, 'I don't know who you are . . .' and that's certainly true or we wouldn't even be having this conversation '. . . but this is my lunch and I'll thank you to leave me to finish it in peace.'

I hear Grafton and Underhill shift behind me. Good lads, they know their cue when they hear it.

'Oh,' I say, 'I'm sorry. You want to finish your lunch, do you?'

'Yes,' he says. 'In peace.'

'Right,' I say, giving him my biggest and best smile, just so he knows how incredibly fucking happy I am. 'Let me help.'

The thing about big men is that they think they're invulnerable. They think weight equals strength. It doesn't. I explain this to Fatty the best way I know how, by hooking my foot around the leg of his chair and pulling while at the same time I shove at his chest. He topples back, the chair breaking underneath him as his fat arse hits the floor.

I grab his plate and sit down on his chest. He has better breasts than that doxy. I wonder briefly about letting him stay on the floor as somewhere comfy for me to relax.

'Here you go,' I say, picking up a piece of cheese and shoving it at his mouth.

He's about to shout and so I drop it in there. I have

enough noise in my head and I don't need him adding to it.

Dirty pig spits it out.

'Manners,' I tell him.

I shove a piece of bread at him to stop him saying anything but he snaps his mouth shut like a naughty baby refusing to be fed. I eat the bread myself while poking Fatty in his eye.

'You *will* eat your lunch,' I say. 'Like a good boy.'

He tries to throw me off and this makes my head pound and the ale army march with even greater vigour.

I draw my sword and hold its tip to his throat.

'You *will* eat your food,' I tell him, 'or I'll cut you a new mouth, understand me?'

He stops struggling, that lovely look of perfect terror settling on him as he realises that not only am I capable of killing him just for sport, I'd actually really *like* to. I'm looking, in fact, for the slightest excuse to do so. He opens his mouth.

'That's better,' I tell him, rubbing the piece of cheese over his face and then dropping it between his lips. 'Hungry boys need their cheese.' This sounds quite absurd to me and I feel foolish sitting on this rotund bucket of shit. My appetite for the game has dis-appeared as quickly as has his for his meal.

I get up, keeping the sword pointed at his throat.

'Goodbye,' I whisper, the ale army pounding its hardest yet as I stand up. How I wish I could find an amusement that would scare them away.

Grafton and Underhill laugh as the fat man rolls onto

his front and scurries from the room on his hands and knees. I haven't got a single laugh left in me. I am brittle. I am sick. I have all the ranks of the ale army marching over me and they're crushing me underfoot.

'Kerro?' says a voice, that of someone who clearly doesn't understand that there's a time and place to talk to me and this is neither.

'Piss off,' I say, 'or I'll show you what I'd have done to him had he not eaten up his meal.'

There is the sound of a coin purse landing on the bar. I decide that just might be the only noise in the world that is interesting enough to quell the rage that's building up inside me.

I open one eye. The purse looks quite full: it certainly sounded nice and heavy.

'Yours if you do a job for me.'

I open the other eye and look at the perfumed servant. He is perhaps a little older than I first thought. Still a little fairy, though.

I reach out, pick up the purse and stick it in my pocket. Best to keep these things safe – you never know in stinking fleapits like the White Hart.

'You don't even know what the job is yet,' he says.

'I am a kind and helpful man,' I reply, 'and people only really employ me to do one thing these days.'

For a moment, just one blessed moment, the ale army ceases marching.

I smile at the dandy, overjoyed at the window of clarity he has brought into my day. 'So who do you want me to kill?'

Twenty-Eight

Marcus Visits the Durwards

Kronos and Grost reappear just as I'm sending Freddie Gluckhaven home. There's nothing the poor lad can do right now and it's obvious that he needs to rest: the shock of what has happened is weighing as heavy on him as anyone would imagine.

'We are going to the village,' says Kronos, mounting his horse, 'on the trail of some coach tracks.'

They gallop back the way they came, leaving me stood alone at the site of our latest death.

I used to love these woods but I doubt I'll ever feel happy in them again. I am a man who has sworn to uphold life, though all I seem to do of late is attend on death. Which makes me think of Hagen Durward and the fact that the Durwards' home lies also in the direction where Kronos and Grost are riding.

A wind rustles through the trees and I let my mind wander. Could there be some connection between these deaths and the exaggerated ageing of Lady Durward? The good lady may be a great deal more alive than Petra, Ann or Sally but the coincidence seems too strong to ignore. I won't send Kronos there, though – not yet, at least: I owe the family a little more tact than that. I should visit myself and see if I can sense something amiss.

While I ride through the forest I think about Hagen Durward and wonder how his bereaved family can look back on him with such a different perspective. The statue in the graveyard labels him a fine swordsman. That he was. It is revealing, however, to note that, unlike on nearly every other memorial you see in that hallowed plot, there is no mention of what he was like as a human being. It is in incised granite or carved wood that loved ones seek to extol the virtues of the deceased. They sing the praises of the lost one as a father, husband or (often saddest of all) child. The Durwards chose to acknowledge the man's skill at killing.

Hagen Durward was not a good man.

Of course, now, seven years later, he was remembered as exactly that. But I remember better. I can recall the bruises glimpsed on young Paul's arms. I remember the look of terror on Sara Durward's face when Hagen howled in pain from his sickbed: it was the look of a girl who twitched to please an aggressor in an attempt to make everything all right before his agony got too much to bear.

I had done my best, of course. I'm a doctor, not a judge of men. Hagen Durward had been confined to his bedchamber for fear of infecting the rest of the family and, with the assistance of a nurse from the village, I had steered him towards death as painlessly and humanely as I could. Nonetheless, the voyage had not been smooth.

The disease had caused Hagen's muscles to cramp,

those swordsman's heavy arms contorting as he writhed beneath the bed sheets, sheets that were stained yellow and pink despite the frequency with which they were changed. His skin had blistered as if it had been pressed against a blacksmith's hot iron. He had bled internally and a hacking cough had sent terrible gobbets of blood across the room to spray on the fine oil paintings and tapestries. Disease has no time for art or social position.

The nurse and I had wrapped ourselves tightly in linens, careful to keep contact with Hagen Durward to a minimum while also providing whatever comfort we could. Which was precious little, judging by the constant screams, curses and attempts by Hagen to injure his medical staff.

Every day I would occasionally step out of the room to get my breath and recharge my strength. I would catch the eye of Lady Durward, forever close by, forever awaiting news. Eventually I couldn't even bring himself to express the usual platitudes: her fear of her husband's imminent death was so overpowering that it was easier to be in the room with the dying man than under her gaze.

At last Hagen died. One final convulsion and a scream that threatened to put out the windows. I had sat in the bedchamber for full half an hour, putting off the inevitable conversation with Lady Durward. Eventually, aware that I could wait no longer, I had stepped outside. She was there as always, standing in the doorway of her room. Her stare had met mine and I had not had to say a word.

'Get out,' she had whispered, stepping inside her room and shutting the door softly behind her.

I made a few pleas to Paul, not least because I was determined that the body should be disposed of carefully. But the son would not go against the edict of his mother. Eventually, Clements, the Durward's butler, was forced to escort the nurse and myself off the premises.

'Apologies, sir,' he said as we descended the front steps, 'but I have a feeling that things will be difficult here for some while.' He was proven to be quite correct. The nurse and I left the house.

I have not been back there since.

At one time the Durwards had been the main power in the area. Now, in these uncertain political days, they were simply the owners of the big house to the north of the village. Since the death of Hagen they had kept themselves to themselves. Occasionally either Paul or Sara would be seen but even then any audience with them would be brief and awkward. They had become a mystery, the family that kept its own counsel.

I ride up the long drive, noting that the grounds are as immaculate as ever. (The Durwards may have kept out of village life but they still provide work for a number of locals, Ed Barrowmund, the groundsman, and his sons included.)

I dismount and, trying not to look as awkward as I certainly feel, I knock on the front door.

Clements answers, as dour and dry as ever. 'Good afternoon, sir,' he says, though I can tell that my arrival has caused him some concern. Does he think my presence will anger his mistress?

'I was just passing,' I lie, 'and thought I'd pay my respects.'

'I'm sure that's most kind, sir.' For a moment he looks as though he may say something else but then a voice calls out from behind him.

'Who is it, Clements?'

Clements steps out of the way, pulling the door open wide, and I step inside to be greeted by Paul Durward.

Paul, much like Clements, cannot quite pretend that he is pleased to see me. He does at least try.

'Dr Marcus.' He smiles. 'A pleasure to see you again so soon. What brings you to our door?'

'I was just passing,' I say again, 'and thought perhaps I should drop in.'

'Just passing?' Paul cannot quite hide his scepticism. 'One can't imagine where you might be heading.' He waves the comment away, as if embarrassed that he even made it. 'No matter – it's a pleasure to have you with us. Do come through.'

He leads me to their drawing room, a refined, colourful room that is bigger than my entire house. I stand, feeling adrift, in the centre of a large rug, wondering quite what I should say next. Perhaps it's best to stay close to the truth.

'I was a little concerned,' I say, 'that I had caused offence the other day. I just wanted to ensure that I hadn't spoken out of turn.'

'Not at all,' says Paul, handing me a glass of sherry that I don't really want. 'Your concern was appreciated, though unnecessary.'

'Good,' I reply. 'Good . . .' My conversation is floundering again already. I pace, and pretend to admire the paintings on the walls: bland pastoral scenes and portraits of austere-looking family members. In the end, Paul saves me further awkwardness by asking me a question.

'I hear that you have visitors,' he says. I obviously look slightly surprised as he feels he has to explain. 'The staff talk,' he says. 'You know how it is.'

'Oh indeed,' I reply, with a smile. 'And they're quite right. An old friend of mine with whom I served during my army days.'

'Really? I'd heard he was foreign.'

'So many of us are if we go back a few steps along the family tree.' I know for a fact that the Durwards have French blood from no more than a couple of generations ago.

'Indeed,' Paul agrees, sipping at his sherry. 'We're all citizens of the world, are we not?'

'I like to think so.'

'It's just a social visit, then?' he continues. 'I had understood he was here due to some medical problem or another.'

'He's not a doctor, though I'll admit he's been helping with the current problems.' I decide there's nothing to be gained by being shy. 'Three local girls are dead,' I say. 'They aged prematurely in a matter of a few seconds.'

'Ah,' Paul replies, 'I had heard something of the sort. Perhaps now I can also see why my mother's condition interested you?'

I hadn't expected such candour but am only too happy to match it.

'Indeed,' I reply. 'I had wondered if there might be a connection.'

'My mother has suffered from grief,' he says. 'Nothing more. It has not been kind to her, it so consumes her that she rarely leaves her room. In fact,' he drains his sherry, 'you might say I lost two parents that day rather than just one.'

'I'm sorry,' I say, unsure how to respond to this announcement.

'Oh dear,' says another voice from the doorway. 'What are we sorry for today?'

It's Sara. She is dressed, as is her wont these days, in gentleman's clothes. I can't say I mind the affectation: she looks rather good in tight britches.

'Nothing, sister,' says Paul dismissively.

'Indeed not,' I concur, feeling it politest to do so. 'After all, who could be sorry in such company?'

It's a lazy piece of empty charm but it serves to lighten the previous mood. I kiss Sara's hand and she gives a slight bow before moving over to her brother and draping her arm around him. There is something a little misplaced in their manner, I note. They act like husband and wife rather than siblings: there is a definite sexuality in their contact. Is this what their isolated life has brought them? A confused and unholy affection?

'And what brings the doctor to our door?' Sara asks. 'Please tell me that nobody's ill.'

'Indeed not,' I reply. 'It is purely a social call.'

'Not to see mother, I'm sure?'

'If she'll see me . . .'

'She won't,' Paul replies. As before, the comment isn't made with any aggression: it's simply a statement of fact.

'Ah,' says Sara, 'what it is to be old. Withdrawn from life, attending on nothing but the grave.' She gives her brother a positively lascivious smile. 'I shall never do it,' she says. 'I shall remain youthful for ever!'

'If only that were possible,' I say, 'this would be a nation of adolescents.'

'Isn't it just that?' she parries. 'Anyway, don't let me interrupt you, I was only coming in for this.' She picks up an aged book from one of the tables.

'Researching how to retain your youth?' I joke.

'Perhaps.' She smiles and holds the book up so that I can read the title: *Witchcraft: The True Science.*

I laugh, for certainly there is no other polite response. 'Do let me know if you have any success.'

Sara just smiles again and strolls out of the room.

'A charming young woman,' I say. The look of discomfort on Paul's face is so obvious that I hardly know what to do. 'I mustn't continue to disturb you,' I say eventually, feeling that escape is the best option.

He doesn't argue. 'A pleasure to see you,' he says, taking my sherry glass – still half-full – and setting it down.

I give a slight bow and step back out into the entrance hall. I can still hear Sara's footsteps on the stairs as she returns to her room. But is that another noise? A creak of a floorboard? Am I being observed by the other member of the household?

'Thank you again,' I say, 'and please do send your mother my best wishes.'

Paul inclines his head, choosing neither to accept nor refute the suggestion, and Clements leads me to the door.

'Be careful, sir,' he says as I mount my horse.

'Careful, Clements?' I ask. 'Of what?'

He shuffles awkwardly and then nods at the sky. 'Has the look of a storm,' he says.

I don't follow his gaze but rather look at the upper storeys of Durward Hall. I can see the ageing face of Lady Durward looking down from one of the windows. That such a woman can have lost such beauty, I think: the cool grey visage that watches me has all the charm of a gargoyle. 'I dare say you're right,' I tell Clements as I turn my horse and head back down the drive.

As I enter the forest I begin to think that he is. A cool wind is pushing its way through the trees and the lazy late-summer warmth that has hung over us all these last few weeks is gone to be replaced by a distinct chill of autumn. Jenny shuffles her feet and takes a couple of sideways steps, as if unnerved by something in her path. Looking through the swirling leaves, I see nothing ahead.

'What is it, girl?' I ask, running my hand across the mare's head. 'What's spooked you?'

The wind continues to build and I'm forced to grip the reins tight as she continues to quiver beneath me.

'Easy,' I say, aware that she may bolt at any moment.

I have no wish to break my neck falling off her during a panicked gallop through the trees.

The sky above me darkens and it's the most damnable thing I've ever seen, as if someone has just leaned over the world, casting their shadow.

'What the devil?' The word feels too accurate in my mouth and I give a genuine cry of fear as Jenny rears beneath me.

The path is no longer empty. Moving through the clouds of leaves, like a hand pulled through water, moves a figure in a long hooded robe. The wind whips at the hood and I catch a glimpse of a full young mouth.

'Sara?'

I feel dreamy. That glimpse of lips somehow seems still sensual even as the storm begins to rage in earnest. I feel myself fall backwards, thrown from the saddle. The world seems to halt. I hang there in mid-air, surrounded by static leaves. Ahead of me, the mare is likewise frozen, a spume of froth whipping from the corner of her mouth.

I try to speak but to do so would need my lips and tongue to move and nothing moves in this impossible world. I am trapped like a character in one of those dreary oil paintings that line the walls in the Durward drawing room.

And yet . . . not everything is bound by these rules. Out of the corner of my eye I can see the robed figure move closer until it is standing just behind me. I can feel its presence, I am aware of a faint scent of violets as it – no, *she* – leans over me. There is another glimpse of lips, red and soft, of a type that I haven't felt against mine for years, and then they are pressed down on me and there is a rush of cold air.

And then I'm riding along the path, the edge of the forest just ahead of me. The trees are calm now, their branches utterly still. The sun is as warm as before and its light and heat settle on my skin as if to brush away the ghost sensation of a kiss that I cannot swear to have received.

I press my hands to my temples, disorientated. I must have passed out, lost consciousness back there on the path and hallucinated the bizarre vision of time standing still. Was there perhaps something in the drink that Paul gave me? Some opiate that robbed me of my senses?

I lower my hands to the reins and a spot of blood hits the perfect white of my gloves. It brings back memories of Hagen's last hours.

I touch my nose, assuming that it's bleeding, but no . . . there is no sign whatsoever of a source for the blood.

I ride home, eager to leave the forest and the memory of darkness far behind.

Twenty-Nine

Clements Fears The Household

One might wonder what sin one has committed to be in service here. Surely I must be being punished? Nobody but a sinner should have to endure Durward Hall for the rest of their days.

It has never been a happy place. Though when Lord Hagen was alive at least the house too was alive with his presence. Now it is a tomb, an echoing series of empty chambers . . . no, not *completely* empty, for certainly this place does not lack ghosts. At night the corridors are filled with the noise of movement, with the sense of someone – something – abroad.

It's a wonder that I haven't gone mad living here. But then, I don't leave, so maybe that's madness in itself. I continue in my duties, caretaker to a dead house filled with the very worst things that a man can imagine.

Perhaps it's honour? I remember young Paul and Sara when they were first born. I have watched them grow as much as – maybe more than – their parents ever did. I have seen them go from scared children to sad adults. There are those who would not countenance their behaviour, would consider them the very worst of sinners. I don't know. I just see two broken people who dare not love anyone else.

Not that it's any of my business. I am here to keep the machinery of the household working: the meals on time, the fires burning, the surfaces clean. If it weren't for me this place would be buried under dust and death. I honestly think I'm the only one who cares enough to stop that happening.

But why do I care?

I couldn't say. It's not as if the Durwards have treated me with any great measure of kindness. To them I am the invisible spirit of the building: I am there to be ignored. Which is as it should be, I suppose. But when a member of the household becomes part of the furniture you no longer hide your feelings from them and I see and hear it all. The tears, the threats, the pain and the violence. I feel tired and dirty just being exposed to it all. I am glad that Mrs Clements no longer has to live here. I think if she were still alive I would lead us out of the front door, never to return. It's never so urgent when it's just yourself, though, is it?

When Dr Marcus visits I don't really know what to do. It's been so long since Durward Hall had guests. My first inclination is to tell him to leave, to run back down the drive before the disease that sits at the heart of this building can place its grip on him. Dr Marcus is a good man – he shouldn't have to be exposed to the atmos - phere here.

I realise, however, that I can hardly say this. If I cannot myself understand the nature of the affliction of the building how on earth can I make the doctor understand? I can tell that he has seen in my expression something of the dilemma. An attentive man, the doctor – comes from examining his patients, I shouldn't wonder. Maybe he can get to the bottom of Durward Hall's malady.

Master Paul's arrival takes my mind off the dilemma and I stand back to let the doctor in. Once the pair of them are in the drawing room I hang back, hoping to catch a few words of their conversation. It is not right for one such as I to eavesdrop, I am aware of this, and yet I cannot help it. It is only as I hear her ladyship's footsteps above me that I withdraw to the kitchens.

I have heard about the young girls dying, of course. I still have one night off a week and sometimes, just to get free of the building, I spend it in the bar of the White Hart. I listen to the old gossips like Clyde Lorrimer, so I know a few of the things that go on outside these four walls. Most days they seem as distant as news of other countries, so trapped do I feel within the confines of Durward Hall, but there is something about these particular stories . . . Perhaps it's because they feel unearthly and infernal. I feel more in tune with the Devil's business.

Once in the kitchen I check on that evening's meal. Cook has made game pie and it looks good. I make a mental note to congratulate her on it: certainly the family won't do so, they have little enthusiasm for her efforts. She deserves better.

Returning through the main house I see that the doctor is leaving already. Perhaps he too has sensed the atmosphere? I see him pause and glance towards the upper floors. It doesn't pay to show curiosity here so I make my presence heard and escort him from the building with a few misguided words of warning. He doesn't understand, of course – how could he? Either I take him fully into my confidence or I let him go. Have I really any choice?

As he rides down the drive I sense movement from within the house and am forced to grip the door jamb to stop myself from falling. Let them not attack the doctor, I think: the doctor is a good man.

'Clements?' comes the master's voice from behind me. 'What's wrong with you?'

'Nothing, sir,' I assure him, catching my breath. 'Just a momentary dizziness.'

He stares at me for a moment and it occurs to me that this is the closest attention he's paid to me for years. Eventually he nods and moves off to the library, leaving me to my duties.

Once I'm alone I crane my head out of one of the front windows and look at the sky. It is darkening and it makes me shiver. There is nothing natural in this weather, I know, and when I hear the sound of doors banging in the corridors above me I am only too aware that something is afoot.

But it's none of my business.

Neither is what lies beyond the cellar door, the only part of the house that is closed to me.

'What they want to go locking that up for?' young Lily, the char asks.

'Never you mind, my girl,' I tell her. But I catch her looking at it and wondering whenever she passes with her brush and beater. It's a curiosity that will do her no good. I'd tell her so, but that would only intrigue her more.

Night falls and the game pie is delivered to the family table, picked at and returned. I take the precaution of disposing of a portion of it before allowing it to be sent back to cook. I wouldn't want her to know that it had been barely touched.

After dinner the house settles into itself and the family retire to their rooms as if even they cannot bear to be abroad in its corridors after dark.

I extinguish the candles and restore everything to its right place, eager to lock myself away in my own quarters.

It's as I am moving towards the stairs that I glance towards the cellar door. I feel curious about what's behind it, just like young Lily. You're a foolish old man, I think as I walk over to it and rest my hand against the wood. There's nothing good that can be gained from this and you know as much, I tell myself.

I ignore my own advice and reach for the handle. Of course it's locked. Satisfied, I walk away. It is only later, when I come to remove my gloves, that I see the white cotton has been stained by blood from the door handle.

Thirty

*Brothers in Blood – The Memoirs of Professor
Herbert Grost: Volume One* (Unpublished)

Kronos and I arrived outside the White Hart Inn just
as the weather looked like it might be taking a turn
for the worse.

'Summer storm,' I said, looking up at the clouds.
Kronos just grunted and entered the inn.

He had followed the coach tracks as far as he'd been
able but they'd petered out on the edge of the woods as
the hardened earth, baked in the sun, was too solid to
retain sign of them. We decided to continue on our way
to the inn and ask whether a coach had been seen
passing. I suspected that Kronos was thirsty. A glass of
wine on top of the skinful we had drunk the night before
might be the best way to settle our stomachs.

It was not a nice place. The sort of tavern where one
went in order to get thoroughly stabbed after imbibing
a little bad beer.

'Wine,' said Kronos, never one for small talk. The
barman brought us each a cup and I looked around.
The place was empty except for the barman and, on
the far side of the fire, three gentlemen of the cut-

150

throat type. These must be the adventurers whom Marcus had mentioned, I realised, the ex-soldiers who had been staying here on their way to opportunities new.

I looked away, not wishing to encourage contact, and stared down at my wine. It was like pond water. I wondered briefly if I might have a more pleasing time were I to drink from the inn's spittoon.

'Did a coach pass this way within the last half an hour or so?' asked Kronos.

The barman, a small, bald, sinewy man who looked like a knuckle in a shirt, glanced over Kronos's shoulder at the three men sitting by the fire. He was clearly scared of his own customers.

'Well?' Kronos asked, impatient as ever.

'Who's asking?' said one of the three men – the leader, I assumed from the fact that he was doing the talking.

He got up from his chair and came over to us. Oh yes, I thought, definitely the leader: he's walking slowly so that we realise it.

He was middle-aged and sported a short beard that suggested laziness rather than fashion. His shirt had once been white but was now the same tobacco-stained colour as the walls. The best thing about him were his boots, knee-length and of fine black leather. Maybe he'd stolen them.

'I said . . . who's asking?' He offered a smile that showed off his teeth in their worst light. Then he spat a spray of tobacco juice onto the floorboards.

'Is there a reason why such information is closely

guarded?' asked Kronos. 'What does it matter to you who we are?'

'It matters,' the man said, glancing at me. His stare lingered, taking in the curve of my back. His grin grew wider. 'Or maybe it doesn't,' he said. 'Maybe I can guess, thanks to your freakish friend.'

'Freakish?' asked Kronos.

'Kerro . . .' said the barman, clearly concerned about where this conversation might lead – though not as concerned as I was.

'Yes,' said Kerro. 'Freakish. Deformed, misshapen. As twisted and ugly as a pig's cock, in fact.' He laughed at this bit of choice wit and his companions joined in as they stepped across the room to join him.

They were just as handsome, and the combined smell of old beer and unwashed flesh now that the three of them were close together was almost over-powering.

'You shouldn't talk about my friend like that,' said Kronos. 'You might upset him.'

'And why would that bother me, my friend?' said Kerro.

'Because then I would be upset too,' said Kronos.

Kerro looked at each of his colleagues and they laughed. He turned back to Kronos.

'As you can see, we're all very scared of you.' He held up his hands and mimed a scream. 'Though it's only fair to warn you that you face three veterans of more battle - fields than you have likely heard of, let alone fought on. I couldn't begin to tell you how many men I have killed, my friend, not because I've lost count but because I slay so readily without the least remorse that I can't say the screams of a single one of them has stuck in my memory. I am a man who kills, sir: it's what I do.' He shrugged. 'Perhaps it's better just to show you.'

He laughed and his hand reached for the grip of his sword. It got there a little after Kronos drew his own weapon. In fact, all three men were too slow – though it took them a moment to appreciate the fact. They stood there, wondering what Kronos had just done.

'I am sorry for the mess, landlord,' said Kronos, taking a sip of his drink. He scowled. 'This is not good wine.'

'What mess?' asked one of Kerro's colleagues just before he fell over dead.

Kerro turned to watch the man fall, then stared in puzzlement as his friend followed suit.

'What did you . . . ?' The faint red line at Kerro's throat blossomed and his stained shirt turned scarlet as the blood pumped. 'Oh,' he said, just before his head toppled back and split the wound in his throat wide. His legs gave way beneath him and he crashed down against a table and a couple of chairs.

However often I see Kronos at work I will never cease to be amazed by his prowess. Two long slashes of his sword and three throats are cut. It all seems as simple to him as breathing itself.

'So,' said Kronos, turning back to the landlord. 'I say again: have you seen a coach pass this way?'

Thirty-One

Carla Practises Medicine

While the rest of them go chasing off to the forest, I stay at Marcus's house and try to make the God-awful pounding in my head go away. I decide – not for the first time – that it would be better if I were never to drink wine again. No doubt I will make this promise again one day, just after I break it.

I am not a girl who is very good with promises, I am the sort of person who likes to be spontaneous and that's easier if you don't burden yourself with a whole list of things you mustn't do.

Take sleeping with Kronos. I had promised myself that I wouldn't do that, either. He's mad, dangerous and not at all the sort of man my mother would be pleased to see me climb into bed with. Which is pretty much an exact list of all the qualities that make a man *worth* climbing into bed with.

Still, I'm angry I did it, probably more because he expected that I would, sooner or later, than because I didn't enjoy it. Because I did. Enjoy it, that is. He was surprisingly considerate. Men as self-obsessed as he clearly is usually act as if they're on their own and it can be a boring and unfulfilling chore sleeping with them. Kronos was not like that. Not only do I have a headache, I am also extremely tired: that last is entirely his fault.

But he is a smug sod and I am rather angry that I have helped sustain his belief that women will fall into bed with him at the first opportunity.

However much fun it was.

And tiring.

Oh, my head . . .

I decide that, as a doctor, Marcus must have something that can make me feel better. Abandoning the cool dark of the stables, I aim for the main house, giving Clyde Lorrimer a smile on my way past. He gives me a funny look in return, as if he knows something that he's not letting on about.

'What's wrong with you this morning, Mr Lorrimer?' I ask, because you never know, it is just possible that he might give a straight answer to a straight question.

'Nothing wrong with me, miss,' he replies. 'Should there be?'

'You just had a look on your face . . . oh, never mind . . .' I am not in the mood to trade words with the likes of Clyde Lorrimer.

'Your master not here, then?' he asks as I'm about to step inside the house.

'I've told you before,' I reply. 'He's not my master. But no, he isn't here – why did you want to see him?'

'I reckon quite a few folk will be wanting to see him,' Lorrimer says, 'on account of what they found on poor old Father Volk.'

Not dead priests again, I think. They're what started me off in the first place.

'What did they find?'

'Reckon I'll not mention that,' he says, a smug look on his face. 'Not until later anyway.'

'Suit yourself.' I really cannot be bothered to play the game, not today.

Inside the house I help myself to a glass of water from the jug left over from breakfast. It doesn't matter how much water I drink today, it drains away as if I'm a plant that's been left in the sun for days.

'Now then,' I say to myself, 'where does a doctor keep his medicines?'

I find under the stairs a large cabinet, filled to the brim with jars, bottles and boxes.

Now I come to my next problem: nothing is labelled at any great length. It simply says what each item is, not what it's for. Which stands to reason, really: why would Marcus feel the need to remind himself how to do his own job at every step?

Mother was a nurse and I try and remember what she used to give people when their heads hurt. This would be easier if *my* head didn't hurt. I start opening jars and sniffing them in the hope that I'll trigger a memory once I smell something familiar.

Then I find the leeches. And drop them. Which is a pain but I hadn't been expecting to stumble across medicine that actually moved.

With a sigh that feels so long and deep it could come from the very depths of the earth, I sink to my knees and start picking up the horrible, wriggling things. A job that I'm still doing when Kronos and Grost appear.

'Making friends?' Kronos jokes. The look I give him is enough to silence any more attempts at humour.

Grost, lovely kind Grost, stoops down to help me. Something has upset him, I can tell: he is very quiet.

'What's wrong?' I ask, putting a hand on his arm.

'Nothing,' he says, quick and petulant, just like a child.

Kronos gazes down at me. 'Why would anyone want to put such creatures on themselves?' he says, looking at the leeches with a sneer on his face.'

'They purify the blood,' I tell him. 'My mother was a nurse – she used them all the time.'

'Really?'

'Oh yes. If you were sensible you'd sit down and let me apply a few now. Why would a warrior not take every opportunity to make himself as fit as possible?'

'I don't know . . .'

'Not scared, are you?'

Which is how I have him sitting in the front room with his shirt off while I stick leeches all over his back. It may do nothing for him but it certainly makes me feel better.

'Did you speak to Lorrimer?' I ask Kronos and Grost.

'He doesn't go out of his way to make conversation,' Kronos admits. 'I don't think he likes me very much. In fact . . .' He squirms as I place another leech between his shoulder blades. 'I get the impression that very few people around here do.'

'At least they don't insult you,' says Grost and I guess this is why he is upset.

'Who insulted you?' I ask and Kronos tells me what happened at the White Hart.

'Am I so repugnant?' Grost asks. 'So terrible to look at that I deserve mockery?'

'Beauty is only skin deep,' I tell him, 'and withers in no time. A good heart is much more precious and it lasts for ever.'

He smiles slightly. 'That's very sweet.'

'My mother used to say it all the time.'

'Then she was a very wise woman,' says Kronos, 'and was worth a thousand of the scum we met today. Besides, don't take their comments to heart, my friend. They were paid to insult you, after all.'

'Paid?' asks Grost.

'Aye, paid. Somebody wanted Kerro and his men to pick a fight with us. They chose the easiest way: they insulted my very best friend. It means nothing, though, they would have said whatever they needed to in order to get what they wanted.'

'But if they were paid to attack us . . .'

'Then someone wants rid of us, which means they feel under threat, which means . . .'

'That we're getting closer.'

'Absolutely! So isn't that worth a few harsh words?'

Grost smiles. I place another leech on Kronos's back. He's covered with them now and they're all dark and swelling. I don't know how they are making him feel but my headache's almost gone.

'Why did you mention Lorrimer?' Grost asks, having

remembered this earlier point in the conversation.

'He was acting strangely earlier. Then he started gloating about something that was found on Volk's body.'

'What?' Kronos asks.

'I have no idea. He wouldn't say, just seemed to feel that it would make people want to ask you questions.'

'Ask *me*?'

I nod.

Kronos gets to his feet, still covered in leeches, and steps outside.

'Lorrimer?' he shouts. 'Lorrimer! Where are you?'

After a few moments the man appears, his axe in his hands. I'm reminded of our initial friendly greeting.

'No need to shout the place down,' he says. 'I'm here. Not that I have to come when you call me, mind.'

'Indeed not,' says Kronos. 'Thank you for doing so.'

Lorrimer shrugs. He looks at Kronos, his head tipped to one side. 'Is there a reason why you never seem to have a shirt on?' he asks. 'Is it too hot for you here in England?'

'I've lived here since I was a child,' Kronos says. 'I am perfectly used to the climate. The cold and wet climate, at that.' He turns around. 'I am having a medical treatment.'

Lorrimer screws up his face. 'Don't know as I hold with that sort of thing. Dirty creatures, ain't they? Live in swamps and marshes – don't know how it's sup - posed to do you any good, having them stuck all over you.'

Kronos nods his head. 'To be honest I'm not sure

what's so good about them myself. I am just doing as Carla says.'

'Ah . . .' Lorrimer replies. 'That girl's doing, is it?'

I'm only on the other side of the window, my friend, I think, and am happy to come out there and put that axe in you if you're going to be rude. But I don't say anything. Kronos is obviously trying to be friendly and chopping people up doesn't help a man do that.

Kronos chuckles and nods. 'I think she's doing it just to be unkind!' he says. 'I think it makes her laugh.'

Lorrimer agrees earnestly. 'I can imagine only too well,' he says. 'There's something wrong with that girl. She was talking yesterday about how she had bitten someone's ear off.'

'Is that so?'

'Aye, and spat it into the undergrowth.'

Kronos rolled his eyes. 'I think she makes things up sometimes.'

Come here and say that, I think. We'll soon see how long it takes to bite off your extremities.

'For example,' he continues, 'she was talking to me earlier about what they found on poor Father Volk's body.'

'Oh yes?' Lorrimer replies, looking nervous.

'Yes,' says Kronos. 'A fragment of cloth, apparently.'

Lorrimer smiles and relaxes slightly. 'She's making it up,' he says. 'Weren't no piece of cloth.'

'No?' says Kronos, sitting down on the large section of tree trunk Lorrimer uses as a bench for chopping wood. 'But they did find something, then? What was it?'

'Ah . . .' Lorrimer realises he's been caught out. What

possible reason can he give for not telling Kronos? 'It were a button,' he says eventually.

'A button? Really? Snatched off the coat of the attacker, we assume?'

'Well, maybe something like that, yes,' says Lorrimer.

'What sort of button?' Kronos asks, getting up and strolling back over towards the door of the house.

'Well,' says Lorrimer, 'a big gold one.'

'I see,' says Kronos, opening the door and sticking his head inside the building. He smiles at us. 'Pass me my coat,' he says. Grost throws it to him and Kronos steps back outside. 'The sort of button you might find on a military jacket like this?' he asks Lorrimer.

'Well, yes, I suppose so,' Lorrimer replies.

'I see why you might want to talk to me about that,' says Kronos, holding up the jacket. He runs his fingers across every inch of the garment, showing that every button is in place. 'Luckily, my coat is not missing a button. Is it?'

This throws Lorrimer, being forced to endorse the idea one way or the other. 'It doesn't appear to be, no.'

'It isn't,' Kronos insists. 'So, wherever the button came from, it can't be from my jacket, can it?'

'I don't know,' Lorrimer says. 'Maybe you had a spare . . .'

'A spare . . .' Kronos nods. 'I don't, as it happens, which is no doubt foolish but there we have it. I am not a very practical man and I often forget things like that. Still, even if I had a spare I didn't know what was left behind so why would I ask you about it, draw attention to it, if it really were my button?'

'I don't know sir, I'm sure,' says Lorrimer.

'I'm not your enemy,' says Kronos. 'I wish you would believe that – it would make things so much easier. If you would only let me get on with my business.'

'Well, with respect, you would say that, wouldn't you?' says Lorrimer. 'If there's nothing else I'd better get on.'

He slings the axe over his shoulder and walks away. Kronos shakes his head and steps back inside.

'At least you found out what he knew,' says Grost. 'That's the important thing.'

'What else did you think was going to happen?' I ask. 'He is not your friend nor is he ever likely to be.'

Kronos nods. 'Nor do I wish him to be, though it would be a lot easier if I didn't get the impression that half the village would be pleased to see the back of us.'

'These are not friendly times,' I tell him. 'Now come here: I think your leeches are full.'

Thirty-Two

What the Beer Brought out of Hollis

And I'm sure I shouldn't talk, being as this is my establishment and I have a reputation to maintain.

I do, too, and I'll thank you to keep your snide comments to yourself unless you want to get very thirsty in this village. There's nothing wrong with my house. I serve a public need and I serve it very well.

Anyway, we had the strangers in here, didn't we? Oh aye, asking whether I'd seen a coach and horses drive past. Well, I hadn't and I would have told him so right enough except I didn't hardly have time. That Kerro and the two dogs that hangs around with him was straight in there and threatening the pair of them, making a mockery of the hunchback and generally spoiling for a fight.

I don't know if you could rightly say a fight is what they got – the foreign gentleman was far too quick for that. You barely saw his sword move!

'Sorry for the mess,' he says and before you know it I've got three dead bodies on the floor of my establishment, all of 'em pumping blood from the throat something chronic. Buckets of it there were, and me mopping like an old woman for full half an hour.

But here's the strange thing . . . I put the bodies out the back, didn't I? Well, where else did you expect me to stack 'em? I didn't have no staff on, did I? Stuck here on my own, I was. So I dumped them outside, next to where I put the scraps for the pigs. Figured I'd deal with it later when I could pop out, you know? Only I didn't have to, did I?

Not ten minutes later, when I'm dumping the water I've used to clean the floor, I find that all three of them have vanished. Not a sign of them anywhere.

Of course they didn't get up and walk! They were as dead as you get, all three of them. Kerro in particular would've had a hard time keeping his head on: a strong wind and he'd have been wearing it on his back like a tortoise's shell. No, they were dead all right, but some-one took 'em away! Now what do you think would make a person do that?

Thirty-Three

Marcus Goes Hunting

By the time I ride into my courtyard I'm feeling more like my old self and am inclined to write off the whole business as a momentary aberration. I have not been sleeping well since Petra Wilkins died. Indeed, I can hardly imagine doing so ever again. When I close my eyes it is to a vision of that fragile face of dust and crumbling teeth. Such images are not conducive to rest. Time eradicates most horrors and I dare say this will be no exception. But for the time being, a great deal has happened and it would be unreasonable of me not to expect it to have some effect. I am a strong man, yes, but not an invincible one. Tiredness, the heat, an unquiet mind . . . is it any wonder that I had a moment of illness?

'Doctor?' Lorrimer nods at me as I dismount. 'Might I have a word?'

'Of course,' I reply, though in truth I'd rather he didn't, the last thing I want is to deal with an imaginary ailment or some irritating matter of housekeeping. 'Come inside.'

Lorrimer shifts uncomfortably at the thought of that.

'I'd rather not, sir, if you please – I'd rather it were private.'

Oh dear God, please tell me it's not going to be one of *those* medical conversations.

He leads me over to the far side of the courtyard, out of sight of the house windows. (It is obvious this is his intention because he keeps looking at them all the time.)

'Well?' I ask, possibly somewhat abruptly. 'What is it?'

'It's your guests, sir,' he says. 'I feel, after what you did for my Mary, I owes you a little consideration, so I'm talking to you man to man, as it were.'

'What's the problem with my guests?' I ask, imagining that Kronos has been clambering on the roof again or practising his swordsmanship in the nude.

'They're not welcome, sir,' he replies. 'Not welcome at all.'

'Lorrimer,' I say, trying not to grit my teeth too hard, 'this is my house and I decide who is or who is not welcome.'

'It's not a matter of your house, sir: we don't want them here in the village. Since they came we have had three girls lost to us and Father Volk gutted like a calf at market. It ain't right . . .'

'No, Lorrimer, it isn't right at all. Both Petra Wilkins and Ann Sorrell died before my guests arrived.'

'With all due respect, sir, we only has their word to go on for that – and their word ain't worth much, in my opinion.'

'Good God, this is ridiculous! You have no reason at all to suspect my friends of being involved.'

'That's not altogether true sir, a button was found near Father Volk's body, a button off a military uniform.'

'A button? Found by whom? I was the one that discovered the body, remember?'

'Indeed I do, sir, and I'm sure you behaved in a proper fashion, no matter what they're saying. It can't have been easy, seeing something like that.'

'"No matter what they're saying"? Why, what *are* they saying?'

Lorrimer shakes his head. 'Don't mind yourself about that, sir, people will talk. I think such a reaction shows grace in the sight of such atrocity – I think no bad of you for it.'

We're getting nowhere and I really have lost the little patience I had. 'Look, Lorrimer,' I say, 'I really have had about as much of this as I can tolerate. I haven't the faintest idea what behaviour of mine you're referring to but might I suggest that you learn to take a little less gossip with your facts? My guests are staying until they or I deem otherwise and it is none of your business – or indeed the business of anyone in this parochial, nonsensical little village!'

And with that I storm off, every ounce of mood improvement that I have felt since my episode in the woods now lost. My head is pounding and my mouth is dry as I step inside my house to find Carla trying to prise leeches off Kronos's back with a spoon.

'You need to use a naked flame!' insists Grost, 'I read it once in a medical textbook . . . or was it a naturalist's guide? My memory fails me . . .'

'You need to do no such thing,' I tell them. 'You need to leave the bloody things alone and allow them to drop off when they are full.' I glance at the veritable pack of the things that the silly girl has unleashed on Kronos's back. 'Or until you are empty, whichever happens sooner.'

'Sorry,' says Carla, looking suitably ashamed.

'Don't worry about it,' I tell her. 'It's the least of my concerns: I have a splitting headache and my handyman is warning me that I should have you booted out of the area because you're not in the least welcome.'

'And we try so hard to be charming,' says Grost.

'Indeed,' I reply. 'Peppering the area with dead amphibians is always appreciated. Thankless buggers, these locals, aren't they, for not appreciating your efforts?' I go to my medicine cabinet and take out a jar of peppermint leaves.

'Is that for your headache?' asks Carla.

'Yes,' I say. 'I intend to make some peppermint tea. Why?'

'No reason,' she mumbles, returning to poke gently at Kronos's back.

I make my tea in silence and then sit down at the table. After a moment I realise there's no need to take my irritations out on them. To do so would be to behave as misguidedly as Lorrimer and the rest of the villagers.

'Sorry,' I say. 'I'm not feeling quite myself.'

'Anything I can do?' asks Grost.

'Thank you, but no. I'm the doctor, after all. I prescribe peppermint tea, a little rest and then copious apologies to my poor house guests who certainly don't deserve my irritable rantings.'

'No apology necessary,' says Kronos.

'And I'm sorry about the leeches,' says Carla. 'I spilled them by accident while I was looking for something to deal with my headache. Then it seemed like fun to put them to good use.'

I smile and pour her a little of my peppermint tea. 'I don't blame you one bit,' I say. 'There's nothing quite so fun as dumping leeches on a man, is there?'

'They go so . . . puffy!' she enthuses.

'So what made you out of sorts?' asks Grost.

I tell them about my meeting with the Durwards and my experience in the forest.

'And you have no memory of what happened?' asks Grost once I've finished.

'No,' I answer, 'none. Though in fairness that's not as unusual as it may sound. I had a patient once who frequently lost chunks of his day. From the moment he got up to the moment he went to bed his life was a series of events with little to join them together. He would keep finding himself somewhere new, in the middle of some business or another, with no memory of how he got there.'

Grost is fascinated by this. 'And yet he would function normally during these lost periods?'

'Absolutely. He was a grain merchant and he would hold entire conversations, conduct financial transactions . . . he was a very successful man of business. And yet he would often forget big chunks of his activities after the fact.'

'I too have experienced something similar,' says Kronos.

'In your case it's the hashish,' jokes Grost. He looks at Carla and me. 'On his worst mornings he can't remember which way on his horse is forward.'

We both laugh and there is a strange atmosphere of friendship – of family, almost. Since this affair started, all sense of comfort or security has been lost to me. Even with Kronos's arrival the problem has persisted, with no obvious solution in sight. Now, for the first time, I find I can imagine us succeeding in our attempts to rid ourselves of this creature.

'And as for Lorrimer . . . They can be a petty bunch here in Padbury but, truth is, they're just scared. Who can blame them? They feel the need to blame somebody and you three are the obvious choice because you're strangers.'

'At least they'll probably think more fondly of us now,' says Grost, 'after Kronos here killed three ruffians in the local inn.'

'You did what!' My headache, which is gently waning thanks partly to the tea and partly to my improving mood, returns with a vengeance. Much more of this and I can visualise my eyeballs being forced from their sockets by the pulsing in my temples.

'They were hired to kill Grost and me,' says Kronos. 'What would you expect me to do? I defended us and apologised for the mess. Besides, from our brief acquaintance, I cannot believe for one moment that they were much loved. Surely they were strangers to the area too?'

Ah . . . It occurs to me now who he is referring to: Kerro and his men. He's right that they will not be missed. In fact, Hollis will probably find it improves business, having got shot of them.

'Wait a minute,' I say, thinking back. 'You say they were actually hired to kill you?'

'I believe so.'

'You believe so . . . why?'

Kronos leans forward and counts the points he makes on his fingers. 'They wanted to know who we were, suggesting that they needed to identify somebody specific. Once they recognised Grost from his . . . erm . . . description . . .'

'He's referring to my hat,' says Grost. 'They recognised it immediately.'

Kronos smiles and continues. 'They were immediately pleased to have met the people they were after. They then proceeded to try and provoke a fight in the most ham-fisted manner possible.'

'A fight that didn't last long, it has to be said,' adds Grost.

'I don't waste my time on amateurs,' Kronos explains, 'I'm a vampire hunter, not an exterminator of idiots. Finally, Kerro was carrying a large purse of silver coins.' He pulls it from his pocket and drops it onto the table. 'If it was his money I refuse to believe that he would choose to spend it on staying at the White Hart Inn.'

'There you are quite right,' I agree. 'The place is a dump of the highest order.' I reach for the coins and tip them out on the table. 'That's a lot of silver.'

'Yours if you'll take it,' Kronos says. 'Call it the hire charge on your stables.'

'Don't be ridiculous,' I tell him. 'I don't want your money.'

'Nonetheless, you'll take it because you're far too much of a gentleman to refuse the gift.'

I open my mouth to argue more but Kronos holds up his hand. 'Please.' I shrug reluctantly and then nod my acceptance.

'Thank you,' he says. 'May I suggest you use it to move to a nicer village? Anyway . . . the point is that we have obviously ruffled the feathers of our prey. They would hardly try and kill us otherwise.'

Grost leans forward. 'And it is worth noting that there's only one family hereabouts who could afford such a payment.'

It takes me a moment but I grasp what he's saying. 'No,' I insist. 'I can't believe it's the Durwards. Lady Durward is in no fit state and neither Paul nor Sara are bad people . . .'

'It interests me that you seem unwilling to call them 'good', however,' says Kronos. 'Tell me what they are rather than what they are not, as a wise woman once said.' He looks at Carla who smiles.

'They are two young people who still struggle under the shadow of their father,' I say. 'They are often unfriendly, awkward and strange. However, I do not believe they are monsters.'

Kronos nods. 'Time will tell, as it always does. For now, might I suggest that we head once more into the forest? Our activities have made our prey uncomfortable thus far, so let us continue in the same vein!'

172

*

Taking a moment to wash my face and refresh myself, I stare into the mirror and look at the ageing man who stares back. There is plenty of grey in my hair, and the usual selection of lines and creases around my eyes, nose and mouth. I look at the skin on the back of my hands. It has the tough, solid quality of skin that has seen all weathers. I am not old, no, but I am closer to that state than I am to being young. It doesn't bother me: I have seen a great deal and lived a full life. I might have wished that I had chosen to share it with someone but that was a situation that never arose and it's too late to regret it seriously now. Would I want to live it all again? Would I want – as this creature that we are hunting so obviously does – a dose of my youth returned to me? I think not. Life, like the silver coins that are now on my bedside table, only has value because it is rare. If there was an endless supply of it what would be the point?

I head back downstairs and we step outside. Lorrimer has vanished, either to take his lunch or because he has left my employ altogether. I'm not sure I care which. Kronos and I saddle up the horses while Grost and Carla fetch several sacks of equipment. When they return they're jangling like mummers and I can only imagine what it is they are laden with.

With Carla sharing Kronos's horse – Of course! Did I not say it was only a matter of time? – we ride towards the forest.

I have no idea what our plan of campaign might be, nor do I care. There is something about Kronos that simply inspires confidence. There always was. In our regiment I think he was, more than anything else, the reason we survived. With his unassailable confidence supporting us, it simply never occurred to us that we could die and we therefore charged across our battle-fields with such inspired confidence that we intimidated the enemy into meeting our high expectations of our victory and their defeat.

Not that any of us were proud of the fighting we did. There are noble battles and then there is the mere following of orders. Our time in Ireland certainly fell into the latter category. It is worrying how easy it can be to do as you're told, to kill those you are ordered to kill and barely question the morality of it. I don't think any of us were bad people . . . We were just simple men who had found ourselves in the business of violence. Some of us – like Kronos – were naturally good at it, some of us – like me – worked hard at it and stayed alive.

At the end of every day we would sit around a campfire, consider ourselves lucky to be alive, and hope that the next day would see us able to say the same.

Kronos returned to a tragedy that altered him – he was always capable of being cold but not the single-minded hunter that he has become today – and I was lucky to be able to turn my battlefield training into something positive. But then, Kronos would probably say the same.

We skirt the edge of the forest and then duck in, dismounting in a clearing just past the boundary.

'It is obvious that the creature uses these woods as its hunting ground,' Kronos announces. 'So today we shall mark out a perimeter, a series of alarms that will allow us to know whenever someone enters here.'

'And how do we plan to do that?' I ask.

Grost reaches into one of the sacks he's carrying and pulls out a length of red ribbon with a small bell attached to it. He shakes the bell and grins.

'Anything we can do to make the vampire's life more difficult is worth doing,' says Grost.

'They're not exactly subtle,' Carla says. 'Red ribbons and bells . . . why not just place a large sign in the middle of the woods saying: "Vampire, we're onto you!" '

'Why not, indeed?' says Kronos, smiling and I realise that, as he'd mentioned during our earlier conversation, he is doing just that.

Of course, you can't string up ribbons through a busy thoroughfare like this without catching a few unintended victims in your trap. The first is Luke Hopkins, who ends up with a ribbon wrapped around his head. Luke is a mild-mannered young man but his hangover puts him in an unreasonable mood and it is with a selection of choice language that he pulls himself free and goes on his way.

Then there is Bill Frimpton, the beer-filled farmer I mentioned to Kronos when I first wrote to him. Bill treats ale like food and I swear one day he will simply burst. He is also not best pleased to find himself surrounded by the ringing of bells and on the business end of Kronos's sword.

'Want to watch what you daft buggers are doing!' he says, pushing his way free. 'I shall have a few words of complaint about this and that's for sure.'

Next there is Katherine Wilkins who treats the affair as a gross personal insult.

'What do you think you're doing,' she asks, 'assaulting decent folk in such a manner?' She looks at each one of us as if we are naughty children. 'I mean,' she continues, 'who do you think you are?'

By late afternoon we're sure that most of the locals are complaining about us, something that pleases Kronos no end.

'The more they talk, the better,' he announces.

Determined to make one last push we split up, each of us with a pouch of ribbons.

The sun is getting low now and the woods take on that delicate quality they have at dusk, as everything begins to lose its edges in the fading light. It reminds me of earlier and I am once again extremely tired. I have started to wonder if my moment of forgetfulness was not something more than simple strain after all. I have felt slightly nauseous for most of the afternoon, that churning stomach one has when one is starving and yet my lunch did nothing whatsoever to settle it. It is an internal itch that seemingly will not be scratched. By now it's making me irritable and I feel greatly relieved as I stretch the last length of ribbon between the branches of a young cedar.

Then I hear the sound of distant bells and for some reason that I cannot easily define it triggers a wave of panic in me. Logically I know it's extremely unlikely to be anything but another false alarm, and yet a chill runs through me and I run towards the noise as fast as I can.

The bells ring again and this time the sound is like a punch to my quaking guts. What is it that makes me react so strongly? I am by no means immune to the idea of a human sixth sense despite the lack of medical evidence: it is another bizarre lesson I learned in the army. Several times we would be resting in camp, most of us asleep and dead to the world, and then a wave of concern would wash through the ranks. A certainty that we were about to be attacked. Some said we must have heard the advancing boots of the enemy in our sleep, others pointed out that there were those who had been asleep who nonetheless became aware of danger long before the sentry heard a whisper. The truth, they said, was that humans could be just as sensitive as animals when put in a situation where it might make the difference between life and death. Perhaps that is the case, perhaps I knew that the ringing bells were not the false alarm they had previously been.

In my haste I don't watch where I am going and the toe of my boot catches in the loop of a tree root as I approach the jangling sound. I tumble to the ground with a pained cry, my head ringing as loudly as those damned bells as it bounces off the hard ground.

The sound comes again and I pull myself towards it, reaching for my sword. My vision is blurred and I realise what an idiot I have been to expose myself to such danger. I catch a flash of a white blouse and hear the sound of a young woman screaming. There is blood. I see it. I even imagine I taste it. Then there is darkness and my last thought is: *I hope one of the others gets here soon, otherwise the latest victim of this thing is going to be me.*

Thirty-Four

Carla Finds Marcus

The last thing I'm expecting is the woman's scream. At first I don't know what to do. After a moment of standing stupidly, holding a handful of those ribbons, my brain starts working again and I run towards the noise.

Of course, I say my brain starts working but, armed only with some small bells, running towards the sound of trouble couldn't ever be classed as clever, could it?

I don't have to worry. The woman's attacker is long gone. She's lying in the middle of a small clearing, staring sightlessly up at the treetops and the sky. Though her attacker may have gone she is not alone. Lying next to her is Dr Marcus, his face pressed against the soil. I pull him onto his back and his eyelids flicker.

'Is it . . . ?'

'Gone,' I tell him. 'What happened to you?'

He's embarrassed to admit that he fell over and as he sits up the thick yolks of several eggs drip from the front of his shirt. There is an upturned basket nearby. The woman must have been carrying it when she was attacked.

'Did you see anything?' I ask him.

The doctor shakes his head as Kronos and Grost appear in the clearing. 'Not a thing.' He looks up to the other two. 'I'm all right,' he says, 'I just fell.'

'You fell?' Kronos rolls his eyes. 'You're supposed to hit it with your sword, not throw yourself at it.'

Marcus gets to his feet, clearly embarrassed. 'I know. I'm lucky I'm able to get back up again.'

'Yes,' I tell him. 'Don't be so hard on yourself.'

He smiles at that but his smile soon vanishes as he moves over to study the girl's body.

'You know her?' I ask.

He nods. 'Not well, but she lived with her family in the village. She seemed a pleasant girl.'

'It doesn't matter whether she was pleasant or not,' snaps Kronos. 'She's dead and we're no closer to capturing the monster that did it.'

He circles the area, staring at the ground. 'A monster that left no tracks,' he says. 'As if our job wasn't hard enough.'

'It's hardly Marcus's fault,' I say.

Kronos stops pacing and nods. 'You are right. Sorry, Marcus.'

'Quite all right,' Marcus replies, 'I don't blame you for being angry.' He looks at me. 'Though thank you for sticking up for me!'

'This just isn't right,' says Kronos. He's pacing again, this time up and down beside the woman's body.

'Of course it isn't right,' says Marcus. 'We have another death we failed to avoid.'

'That's not what I mean,' Kronos says. 'Look at her!

It's different again. She is not preternaturally aged, nor has she been eviscerated like the priest.'

'She is a much more traditional victim,' says Grost. 'A wound to the neck and a complexion so pale that she can only have got it by losing several pints of blood.'

'And the flowers!' adds Kronos. 'Look at them.'

I squat down and realise that the entire carpet of grass and flowers beneath the corpse has withered in a large circle. If you take the dead woman's body as its centre, the diameter stretches some twenty feet. 'It's all dead,' I say, rather needlessly.

'Surely it can't be another one,' says Grost. 'Three vampires?'

'Is it not more likely,' Marcus asks, 'that it is the same vampire that is learning to alter its method of feeding?'

'Not possible,' explains Grost. 'That would be like a fox learning to fly so he can gobble up sparrows. Each vampire is restricted to its specific form of feeding – it can't just swap when it feels like it.'

'Oh,' says Marcus. 'Then, like you, I am at a loss to explain it.'

Kronos sighs. 'Put her on your horse. We must take her back to the village. Her family must be told what has happened to her.'

Marcus nods but it's plain that he has no great desire to do anything of the sort. Can you blame him? Yet again he will be the source of bad news. His reputation, already battered, is about to take another great blow.

He drapes her as ceremoniously as he can, across the front of his saddle, and we ride slowly through the forest and down the main road that leads directly to the village.

We are spotted almost right away. A small boy runs ahead to tell his parents about the strange people riding towards them. The strange people with a dead body to deliver.

'Her family live on the far side,' says Marcus. 'Small house, second to last on the road.'

'Could we not have looped round?' I ask. 'So we didn't have to ride right through the middle of everybody.'

'They have a right to see,' he replies and I realise he has got to the stage now where he feels he deserves every bit of this bad fortune. Marcus has sunk very low indeed.

'What's happened?' comes a voice just as we're passing the churchyard. 'Who's been hurt.'

Marcus looks up, recognising the man. 'Stephanie Maginn,' he replies. 'We found her dead in the forest.'

The man who had spoken stops in his tracks and shakes his head sadly.

One by one the villagers begin to appear from their homes, walking slowly, staring at us and our cargo as if dazed, confused by this turn of events.

Someone steps forward. He doesn't move confi-dently. He is a reluctant spokesman, inched forward by the crowd. We cannot pass now and are forced to stop, there in the middle of the road.

'Get out of our way, Hollis,' says Marcus.

Hollis, I think . . . which one's . . . ? Ah yes, the landlord of the White Hart.

'I don't think so, Marcus,' he replies. 'I think you should be turning around and leaving. None of you are welcome here.'

'We have to take this poor girl to her parents,' Marcus says. 'That's our duty and I'll thank you to let us perform it.'

Hollis shakes his head. 'You ain't got no duty,' he says. 'Not here.'

A couple of people walk up to Marcus's horse and drag Stephanie's body from it. He doesn't stop them.

The body is dealt with as if it were nothing but a sack of grain. It bounces on the ground as they pull it from the horse, and it is then dragged, its legs splayed and the head lolling stupidly on the neck, up the road and into the crowd. After a few moments there is a strangled cry of grief and I'm guessing that the Maginn family are present and have just been reunited with their daughter.

'Now turn around and get out,' says Hollis. 'And be damned grateful we're letting you do that.'

'Grateful?' asks Kronos. 'If I required gratitude in order to do my job then the world would be a much more dangerous place. Still, this is the first time I have been met with such obvious stupidity. I am here to rid you of a plague, to destroy a monster who lies at the very heart of your community. I am not the one to fear. Look instead to whatever it is that takes your daughters, kills your priest. I can understand your anger, I welcome it, but let it point in the right direction! Save your hatred for the creature that deserves it!'

'I've seen a monster in action these past few days,'

says Hollis. 'He killed three men in the blink of an eye and then left me to dispose of the bodies.'

'Those men wished to kill us,' explains Kronos, 'so as to get us out of the way.'

'From where I'm standing,' says Hollis, 'that's not so bad an idea.'

There's a general cheer of agreement for that and Hollis is bolstered by the people's approval, his chest swelling and his head lifting at a more confident angle.

'So you have two choices,' he says, in his new, more confident tone. 'You either ride out of our village now, never to return, or we'll pull you from those horses and make sure you never leave. Which is it to be?'

Kronos gives a low growl of irritation. This is the last thing he needs. Are three vampires not enough for him to fight? Does he have to contend with the whole town as well? 'One last chance,' he says. 'Help me to face the creature that is killing your people.'

A murmur runs through the crowd. It is not the sound of reasoned consideration, rather a crescendo of unthinking public opinion, the wave that will drive us out once the creators of the noise have reached their peak of anger.

'We need to go, Kronos,' I say. 'Now.'

'She's right,' agrees Grost. 'They're about to turn nasty.'

I look at Marcus, aware that he has said nothing since Stephanie's body was dragged from his horse. 'Marcus?' I ask, wanting his assent. Slowly, he nods. We turn around and ride away, the crowd cheering behind us as we leave the village.

Thirty-Five

Paul Durward is Jealous

I am not a man of words. I despise polite chit-chat and dinner-party waffle. I am not a sociable man. Those things I leave to Sara.

She has always been the stronger of the two of us. When father was alive, she took her beatings with far more grace and strength than I could ever manage. I would always cry and beg. She simply adopted a calm look, a serenity, and managed to endure.

'You must step outside yourself,' she would say to me later as we curled up together in bed. 'Let your mind go somewhere else. It doesn't matter what they do to your body then because you can't feel it.'

I would try to master the art of this, lying there in the dark, trying to push my mind out of my body and down along the corridors of the house. I never succeeded: my flesh was just too heavy.

Then father died and things became very different.

Mother retired to her rooms and now leaves them rarely. It is a terrible part of the house to visit. She will not countenance the curtains being drawn so you stumble in the darkness, choked by the oppressive, airless atmosphere. Mother does not like the world to enter: she inhabits a suffocating, dark place.

'You should leave her to it,' Sara says. 'She's made her choice – there's no need for us to be dragged down with her, is there?'

'She's our mother,' I reply. 'We should remain faithful to her.'

'She's an old woman, getting more and more mad as the days go by.' Sara smiles and stretches out across the sheets like a reclining cat. I watch her muscles tense and then relax into place – she is a wonderful thing to observe. A beauty that strikes me utterly dumb. 'I don't think I shall ever grow old,' she announces. 'I can't abide the thought of losing who I am, having it all crumble away, body and mind.'

'You will always be perfect,' I tell her, running my fingers across her stomach, a smooth plain of delicious cream-coloured skin.

'Yes,' she agrees, 'I think I shall.'

I don't know why Marcus has suddenly started taking an interest in us. I do not blame him for the death of our father (even if I did I couldn't in all honesty hate him for it: I hated my father and I am glad he's dead) but I have no time for the doctor's company. Does he wish to assuage his guilt? Will he pester us until mother condescends to meet him? To forgive him? He will have a long wait if so.

I can sense an undercurrent in the things that Marcus says. A suspicion. Can he believe that the deaths in the village are somehow linked to us? If so, what has made him think so? Do we not keep ourselves to ourselves?

How are we involved in village life? Other than providing a modicum of work and money for the villagers we are a separate country up here, a distant nation set apart by stone walls and social class. What brings him to our door?

'He has no idea,' Sara assures me when I raise the matter with her. 'People always look up when they are confused as to the reasons for something, never down. They always want to blame the person who is more important than them. It is a chain of recrimination that leads to God and therefore to no answers whatsoever.'

'You believe there is no God?'

She laughs. 'Don't be silly. Of course there's a God, but our business is none of his.'

I think about this for a while and then decide that there's no peace to be had in such thoughts. Instead I listen to her sleep and let the calmness of her breathing carry me away to where thoughts have no weight.

The next day I feel better about things, no longer weighed down by concerns that lead nowhere. Let them think what they wish, I decide: it's their problem, not mine.

My comfortable attitude is threatened by the behav-iour of two of the servants. We have a limited retinue these days. Our needs are few and we host no dinners or balls. Clements has been with us since before I was born and he has always been a perfect member of the household. He is quiet, fastidious and seems to hold no serious opinions of his own. Such attributes make him almost invisible and therefore as perfect as a servant can be.

Over the last few days, however, he has become more obtrusive. He seems nervous, suspicious even, as if he knows something about the household that I do not. Something important. I wish I could confront him with it but in truth I don't know what to say, how to express my dissatisfaction. One can only hope it is a passing phase.

The other manservant, the footman Blake, is a different matter entirely. I have never liked him. I dislike his easy manner and his handsome face. He is one of those men who coasts through life on looks and charm. I have frequently noticed Sara looking at him appreciatively, even talking with him, enticing him and flirting with him. It is Sara's way, I know. I dare say she would not act on these apparent interests but her exhibiting them is more than enough to anger me. He is a servant, not someone who should be encouraged in such a way. Of course this affects his behaviour. He is becoming altogether too confident: he moves through the house as if it were his own. I have even spotted him walking around upstairs, despite the fact that his duties should restrict him to the lower levels. When I challenge him on his presence he has the damnable gall to smile at me, as if I am the one speaking out of turn.

'I'm about my mistresses' business,' he says, 'and am sworn to secrecy.'

I was quite apoplectic with rage at such an imper - tinent reply and am all for having the man sacked. It is, of course, my sister that dissuades me from doing so.

'It is so hard to find good servants these days,' she says, 'and we would be worse off without him.'

I can't help but feel that she is wrong in this opinion but, as always, she is able to turn me to her will. It doesn't stop me disliking the man, however, and watching him closely.

'You're just jealous,' Sara says.

The fact that she's right keeps me awake for some hours.

Thirty-Six

Brothers in Blood – The Memoirs of Professor
Herbert Grost: Volume One (Unpublished)

I t was not an easy night.
I cannot say this was the first time that our business
brought us in headlong collision with the consensus of
public opinion. We are rarely welcomed. Indeed, I am
reminded of the Lincoln Vampire, where the creature
had managed to place the majority of the town in its
employ. We nearly swung from the gibbet that time,
too: people rarely love a vampire but when its
patronage keeps food and drink on the table they are
more often willing to turn a blind eye than you might
imagine. These were hard times.

I think it was Marcus's mood that affected Kronos
more than the attitude of the villagers. Kronos is not a
sociable man and he really does not care a great deal if
people like him. He recognised, however, that Marcus
could not say the same. The doctor had taken to village
life, had enjoyed the feeling of being part of its
community, one of its number. To have them turn on
him *en masse* was hard on him.

I tried to talk to Marcus several times over dinner,

reassuring him that once the vampire was routed out he would find his position returning soon enough to the *status quo ante*.

'It is only fear that makes people stupid,' I told him. 'It makes them close up together like a pine cone against the rain. As soon as the danger is over you will find them an apologetic bunch, I'm sure.'

Marcus simply shrugged and busied himself with eating his lamb stew.

He had retreated into himself, as surely as the rest of the village had. He was scared and uncertain. He just didn't have the easy option of blaming his feelings on us.

'Do you think they'll come after us?' Carla asked. 'Are they angry enough to do that?'

'Angry enough, perhaps,' I said. 'But tales of how swiftly Kronos dispatched Kerro and his men will hold them back for a while. We might not be able to fight them all but nobody wants to be among the first few to fall before we do.'

'It's so ridiculous,' she said. 'Why do people never know what's best for them?'

'If they did,' I replied, 'I don't believe they would be human.'

Nobody was inclined to stay up late. Marcus was the first to go to his room, the strain of the day showing clearly on his face. He prepared himself a draught to help him sleep and then retired. Kronos and Carla went next and I hung back for a little while, wanting to afford them a little privacy.

I needn't have bothered. When I entered the stables a

short time later, Kronos was locked in the coach and Carla was lying on the straw, staring up at the ceiling.

'I don't know how you do it,' she said as she heard me join her. 'To always be fighting, always having to watch your back. It's no life.'

'Perhaps not,' I replied. 'But it's the only one we have.'

Thirty-Seven

Morris Blake Decides to Act

Darling Nell,

It has been an eventful few days. I wish I could report that Kerro had expelled our troublesome visitors from the area but I'm afraid to say they attacked him viciously and he and his men are now dead. I cannot help but feel some remorse at this – it was, after all, me that hired them in the first place. True, I was acting under orders; nonetheless my conscience pricks me.

As indeed does the lack of reward. All has been silent on that front, despite my proving myself as efficient and trustworthy as any could ask. But then things are afoot here, I have no doubt of that. Lily, the char, went missing this morning and nobody can explain it.

She was – as her position demands – working her way through the rooms, cleaning and straightening (though given how most of the rooms stay empty morning through night I can't think it's a hard task).

At a quarter to nine we heard a scream coming

from the entrance hall and Clements and I ran to see if we could assist. I cannot speak for Clements but I was of the opinion that the stupid girl had most likely caught her hand on something, maybe pricked herself while cleaning one of old Master Hagen's swords, or catching herself on some clumsily broken glass. She was not the brightest coal in the fire, young Lily, and it would not have been the first time she had caused disruption through her own carelessness.

On entering the hall, however, we found it quite empty. Her brush and bucket were there, waiting patiently for their owner to return and collect them. She never did.

We searched the house from top to bottom – all bar the cellars but she cannot have got in there: they are kept locked and not even Clements has the key. There was no sign of her!

Where can she have gone to? What would make her simply run away like that? It is a mystery, my love, and one I don't mind admitting has left me feeling uneasy.

Clements is off-colour, too: his usual calm serenity has been replaced by a nervous sense of anticipation. He twitches when you talk to him, flinches if you make a loud noise near his person. I cannot imagine what it is that he is expecting to happen but clearly he doesn't look forward to it!

None of which events has helped an atmosphere that was hardly pleasant to begin with. I have resolved to address matters immediately. Either I will see my due reward for my silence and loyalty or I will work elsewhere. I miss you my darling Nell, and cannot bear to be parted from you any longer.

Wish me luck!

Your ever faithful, loving,

Morris

Thirty-Eight

Clements Hopes he is Wrong

So now they have taken Lily. And meanwhile I stand by and do nothing. What sort of terrible coward is a man who does that?

Lily can have harmed no one. She was nothing but a silly, sweet, naive little girl. How could she have stood against a soul?

Of course, Blake believes that she has simply run away. Dropped her tools and run from the house, never to return. How I wish that might be the case. Still, why would she ever do such a thing? Fear? Did something scare her so much that she ran from it? That is certainly possible in this house, a building packed full of horrors. But then, if you ask me, Lily did not leave the house at all.

She had been working in the entrance hall and if the silly girl had one weakness it was curiosity. Had she not asked me, time and again, about the locked door to the cellars? Had I not tried to distract her from her enquiry? I think today her curiosity got the better of her. She placed her brush and bucket down – no doubt she checked to see if there was anyone outside who might interrupt her – then she moved to the cellar door and tried the handle. It would not have opened for of course, it is, as I say, always locked. But somehow she was taken: at that moment her curiosity damned her for good.

I know this. I know this because I know people better than Morris Blake does. I also saw something that he did not. I saw three thin lines of red on the floor in front of the door. Three narrow streaks. Of the sort that might be left if a person had been dragged into the darkness beyond, one bloodied hand trying to secure a grip on something as they went.

Poor Lily.

And now I know I can no longer stand by and let these matters persist. I said before that if my wife were still alive then I would have taken us both from this place. This is true – I would not have left her in danger here for all the world. But she is not here. She was taken from me years ago and in her departure I let her take a little of what it was to be me. I let her take some of my strength. Well, no more: she would not have wanted that. She would have wanted me to ensure that those placed in my care were looked after. Lily was in my care. And now she's gone. I will stand it no longer.

I wait until the household is asleep, the candles extinguished, the corridors cool and empty of all but ghosts and the distant sound of breathing. I light a candle of my own and I make my careful way out of my room. I have kept my feet bare, the better to move silently, and the stone floor chills them with each step.

Even in summer this damned house will not warm itself.

I can hear voices and for a moment I consider returning to my room. The speakers are angry but are trying to remain unheard. One of the voices is that of Morris Blake . . . who could he possibly be arguing with up here? I hesitate on the landing. Should I investigate? No. Let there be only one mystery at a time.

I make my way downstairs, and into the kitchens. The air is filled with the smells of the earlier evening meal. Smoked haddock. It was, as usual barely appreciated by the household but I congratulated cook nonetheless. She is a good woman, a fine woman. She reminds me of the dear, lost Mrs Clements, I realise. That is why I am always so defensive of her. In my own ineffectual way.

I search the drawers in the kitchen for a decent carving knife, something with a bit of weight to it and a sharp blade. I find the perfect example, holding it up to the candlelight so that the flame flickers in its steel. There is comfort to be had from the image.

I unlock the back door and head outside. We keep a selection of tools for both the garden and the house in a small outbuilding at the rear to deal with any minor repair work. I take a hammer and chisel, drop them into the pockets of my robe and return to the house.

I lock the back door behind me (I may be about a bad bit of business but I don't altogether ignore my duties) and head towards the entrance hall.

Inside I draw back the curtains so some light can enter. The better I can see, the easier the job will be.

I place my candle as close to the cellar door as I can manage, balancing it on a small bookshelf filled with unopened volumes of poetry and books about wild flowers. The sort of books that every affluent household owns but few bother to read.

What about the noise? I have not thought this business through.

I remove my shirt and wrap it around the head of the hammer so that it will muffle the sound of it striking.

Placing the blade of the chisel against the lock of the door, I make several slow, deliberate blows with the padded hammer to force the wood away from the bolt. There is the noise of splintering, tearing wood but I do not think that it is loud enough to carry. Metal against metal would have resounded throughout the building – this is delicate by comparison and will not rouse the sleeping household.

It takes me ten minutes or so to get the door open, working carefully and quietly.

I pick up my candlestick and leave the hammer and chisel on the bookshelf. Holding the carving knife firmly in front of me, I begin to descend the stairs on the other side.

It stinks down there, as might well be expected given how rarely it is aired. Still, the smell is not just of dust and damp. My father worked as a butcher and I know the coppery smell of blood when I smell it. There is something dead down here and I am very much afraid that it will be Lily.

There is a movement in the darkness to my left, a

scuffling of feet. I turn the light of the candle towards it and hold the carving knife out in front of me.

'Come out, you terrible thing,' I tell the darkness. 'Let us have an end to you.'

Thirty-Nine

Marcus Feels the Years Fall Away

The night passes badly. Whenever I close my eyes I find my thoughts back in the forest, trapped in a world where time refuses to move forward. Even when I do sleep I dream that I am still out there, held in mid-air as the woods come to life around me. I can hear the birds in the trees, chattering and pecking at the insects that infest the wood. I can hear the creatures that burrow in the soft earth, snuffling and barking and sucking on worms. I am the only living thing here caught in this trap and, as the instigator moves closer, I hear the rustle of her robe as she lifts it up over my face and swallows me into her chilling darkness.

I wake at first light with a head that feels as though I've been drinking. I step groggily to my sideboard so I can splash some cold water on my face and try and bring my thoughts back to life. As the water hits my cheeks, my head pounds and I make eye contact with myself in the mirror. What I see freezes my hands in mid-gesture.

Yesterday I had looked at my face in this very mirror. I had looked upon the features of a man who had lived a good deal of life. There is no trace of that life in the mirror before me. I know the face I'm looking at, know it very well – but I haven't seen it for a good thirty years. The young man I look at has yet to go to war, has yet to leave home. That young man has his whole life ahead of him. And he shouldn't exist . . .

'Kronos!' I shout, pushing my way out of my bed-chamber and running down the stairs. I lose my balance and tumble down the last few steps. It doesn't matter: I barely hurt myself – a young man can take plenty of knocks without it setting him back.

'Kronos!'

I run outside, and as the sun hits me I scream, my skin searing as if it had been touched by flames. 'Kronos!' I fall to the dusty ground of the courtyard, unable to go on.

I wrap my arms around my head, trying to cover my face from the sun's light. I feel hands gripping my shoulders and I'm dragged back into the house. I actually black out for a while and the next thing I know I'm sitting at my kitchen table staring at Kronos, Grost and Carla.

'What's happened to him?' the girl asks.

'He has been turned,' says Kronos. 'He is one of them.'

'I don't understand,' I tell him. 'I just woke up and I was . . .'

'Years younger,' says Grost. 'Rejuvenated.'

'But I don't know how . . .' I insist. I pull my shirt from my neck. 'I haven't been bitten or anything. I'm just . . .'

'One of them,' Kronos repeats. He steps back out into the courtyard.

'Where are you going?' Carla asks. But he doesn't answer her. He returns quickly, a length of rope in his hands.

I look at that rope, then at Kronos, at the ferocious determination in his eyes.

'Is there nothing else to be done?' I ask.

'Nothing,' he replies. 'I wish there were.'

'What are you talking about?' asks Carla, her voice getting louder as she loses her temper.

'I'm afraid Dr Marcus is beyond saving, my dear,' says Grost. 'there is only one kindness that we can offer him.'

It takes Carla another few seconds to realise what is going to happen. 'You can't be serious!' she shouts. 'You can't kill him!'

'That remains to be seen,' says Kronos. 'We don't know how, certainly. Every vampire's bloodline is different and they are all extremely hard to kill. What works on one won't necessarily work on another.'

'I suppose that is some consolation,' I say. 'I can help you after all. I can help you figure out how to kill this thing.'

Carla looks at the three of us in disgust. 'I want no part of this!' she shouts and walks out. I'm glad – she is a lovely girl and I certainly wouldn't want her to see what must happen next.

'Right,' I say. 'Shall we begin?'

We get the easy options out of the way first: the holy water and the herbs. They have no effect, beyond the garlic making my eyes water.

With sadness, Kronos ties the rope around my

neck, throwing the other end over one of the ceiling joists.

'Forgive me,' he asks before yanking the rope tight.

I swing by my neck and I can hear the little bones snap, the muscles tear. My head floats as my breath is stolen away and stars dance in front of my eyes. I hang there for some time. Eventually we all accept that I cannot be killed by hanging.

Kronos lowers me back into my chair and uses the rope to tie me down. 'I have to do this,' he says. My throat is too sore for me to reply. I try to nod my head but the muscles there are not quite healed and my neck refuses to do as it's told.

Next comes the sword, pushed into my heart. I can feel the steel inside me, an intruder in the flesh. It hurts, it burns, but it does not kill me.

The steel is removed and the wood comes next. I can feel splinters peeling off it as the stake is wedged into me. And still I do not die.

Kronos fetches the axe from outside and without a pause, presumably so I don't have time to feel scared, swings the blade at my throat. There is the most awful noise of tearing cartilage and then silence as my head topples back across the floor. I am left to stare up at the ceiling, my mouth wide open and unbreathing – for I have no lungs to breathe with. But I am not dead.

Kronos places my head back on the stump of my neck and I then endure the most bizarre sensation as the skin glues itself back together. Being a medical man I can visualise the sight of it better than most. I can imagine the windpipe healing, the vertebrae joining back together, the nerves knitting up. I certainly know when that last happens as the pain is almost unbearable. I say that as one who has yet to endure the next torture: fire.

Grost looks out of the window, unable to meet my gaze as Kronos splashes me with oil from the lamps and then sets light to me. The sound as the flames encircle me – a giant handclap with me between the palms – is deafening and it distracts me for a short moment before the heat and pain take hold. I try not to scream, thinking of poor Carla, no doubt still within earshot, but the pain is too much and I let loose a loud moan as my skin bubbles and cracks. The smell of my hair aflame would be enough to bring tears to my eyes if I still had eyes to weep with. I wish the flames were hotter, wish they would burn quicker. Eventually the pain stops when the fire has burned the sensation away. I am able to watch my body darken, the skin turning brown then black like that of a hog left too long to roast on a spit. I try and move but the muscles are too damaged and all that I manage is to twist slightly, a loud cracking noise telling me that something on my left has snapped. Then my hearing goes and there is no more sensation at all. Is this it? Is this death? Can this finally be the end?

I am nothing more than thought – and that thought concerns the Durwards. Am I wrong in my opinion of them? Does the answer lie in fact with Paul and Sara?

I have no idea how much time passes but I'm startled by a whining noise that resolves into a voice.

'. . . Think he's returning . . .' It's Grost's voice. 'It didn't work.'

After the sound comes the pain as the skin grows soft once more and rejuvenates.

My eyes are among the last organs of sense to be restored and I peel open gummy lids to see Kronos and Grost staring at me.

'It's not fire, then,' I say and the sound of the words is bizarre in my ears. I realise that my tongue and lips are still re-forming.

'No,' Grost replies. 'I'm sorry, but it's not fire.'

He leans over me, and suddenly there is a pain like no other I've thus far experienced.

'Kronos!' Grost pulls back and they both stare at my cheek.

'What is it?' I ask.

Kronos reaches down and touches the silver crucifix that Grost wears. 'This burned your face.'

Kronos yanks the pendant free and holds the tip of it against my other cheek. The pain is unbelievable! I thrash against my bonds, desperate to pull away, unable to bear the agony a moment longer.

'The crucifix,' he says.

'Wait!' I reply, struggling for breath. 'Is it the crucifix or is it the silver?' I see a look that is almost embarrass - ment cross his face. 'Some bloody doctor you'd make,' I say. 'If you want an accurate diagnosis you have to rule out everything.' I nod towards the fireplace. 'Pair of candlesticks, a gift for my services from a man who had more silverware than money. Try them.'

Kronos walks over to the mantel and lifts one of the candelabra. They are big, heavy affairs – worth a good deal of money, I have no doubt. If my suspicion is right

I might yet have cause to be thankful that I never sold them.

Kronos presses the metal against my face and the pain is, once more, excruciating.

'There,' I say, when I can speak again. 'Might I suggest that you melt them down into something useful?'

'Marcus . . .'

'Oh, shut up,' I laugh. 'You never were cut out for sympathy. Just promise me you'll kill the bastards.'

He nods. 'I promise, my friend.'

Out of the corner of my eye I can see Clyde Lorrimer peering through the window. Oh, I think, this isn't going to look good.

Then Kronos swings one of the candelabra right at my . . .

Forty

What the Fear Brought Out of Clyde Lorrimer

If only you'd seen it. After everything he'd done for them, the way they killed him.

He were tied down and all – they weren't taking no risks. I can understand that sort of thing from the hunchback, I mean, how difficult can it be to fight a hunchback? He'd want to even up the odds a bit, wouldn't he? But the other one, the foreigner . . .

Tied him down, they did, and then brained him with one of his own candlesticks. *Bosh*. Blood and brains everywhere. And Dr Marcus always had had a lot of brains so you can just imagine . . .

Yes, thanks, Dudley, I will just have one more. It's my nerves, see? Shot to bits they are after having seen what they done.

I don't know what made them do it. Maybe they meant to rob the place, or maybe they're just sick in the head, they just like doing that sort of thing. You never can tell. I remember a friend of mine telling me about a woman over in Gloucester, the things she did to men with an ale horn . . . some people just aren't right.

So what are we going to do? That's the thing, ain't it?

We can't just let them get away with it, we should get over there and give them a little of what they gave old Dr Marcus. I mean, Marcus was a good man, I'll always remember how he looked after my wife . . .

What are we going to do?

Forty-One

Carla Learns A Lesson

I can hear Marcus scream and however much I squeeze my hands over my ears it doesn't block out the images in my head. I know he is dying, and dying badly, as Kronos and Grost torture him to death.

I understand that they think they're doing the right thing – perhaps the only possible thing – but the willingness with which they accepted the task is what hurts. Neither of them even tried to offer another solution. The man who had once been their friend and host was now no more than a dangerous animal to be slaughtered by whatever means necessary. Theirs is a determination that I cannot share, it is the the single-mindedness of the zealot, a cold, narrow view that cannot fail to remind me of the most terrible man I have ever known and of what he did to my mother.

It is my hope that one day we will be able to look back on the days of the Witchfinder and wonder to ourselves how such a thing could have come to pass. How we could have been so stupid, so frightened as to not only believe his claims but encourage them.

He and his colleague John Stearne came riding into

our village at the beginning of spring four years ago.

We were just waking up from the winter, welcoming the warmer winds and the damp thaw as a new chance at life. The village was exposed and that year the cold had been particularly harsh. A lot of livestock had suffered and a couple of the older residents had died. The first, Jeremy Bates, had been ill for some time and the general consensus was that if the cold hadn't done for him then something else would have. Old Mother Langley was different. Her death had the sort of mysterious touch that small villages love, a little fuel for the gossip fires. She had been found on her front step, kneeling and with her hands raised in prayer, frozen solid. What had happened to her? The gossips wondered if it had just been the cold or had some evil spirit done for her? Evil spirits were a popular catch-all for anything that stayed unexplained. If the cows weren't milking as well as they ought then evil spirits had infected their teats. If the corn crop was short, evil spirits had worked their way between the rows and soured the seed.

If anyone could make profitable use of this sort of small-minded lunacy it was Matthew Hopkins.

He was a charming man. If anything, that was his worst feature. He conveyed his lies and sadism with such gentle conviction that they were hard to dismiss. If he told you that the Devil was walking the streets of your village or town, if he told you that evil spirits were in residence, you would nod wisely and ask what you could do to help.

Also, people don't like to believe that death can be

random. They like there to be method and reason. If you ask me, people just die and sometimes bad things happen to good people, I honestly believe that . . . It marked me out as very strange indeed.

'Describe how you found this woman,' Hopkins asked, once the story had come to his attention. He had no shortage of eager witnesses: people were desperate to tell him, whether they had actually seen Old Mother Langley in her icy genuflection or not.

'This is no ordinary death,' Hopkins announced in the end. And of course he would say that, for there was nothing that he or Stearne could gain from an 'ordinary' death and, above all, they were greedy men. Greedy for power and all the riches and adulation it could bring.

And so the investigation began. What could Old Mother Langley have seen that made her fall to her knees in the cold? What infernal sprite had paid a visit to her that day and, more importantly, who was its human agent?

Stearne was the more visible of the two. While Hopkins kept to his room at the inn, his accomplice walked the roads and knocked on the doors. I never understood why people didn't see him for what he was. Hopkins was charming, yes, but not so Stearne. When I opened our door to him his eyes crawled over me like spiders disturbed from their nest, scuttling for some - where to hide themselves.

'Good morning,' he said, though not to my face. 'My name is John Stearne, I am investigating the unusual death of Old Mother Langley.'

'Nothing unusual to it,' I told him, still young enough

then not to have learned to guard my tongue. 'It was cold, so she froze.'

'You obviously are not aware of our latest discoveries,' Stearne said as he pushed past me into the house. 'We found signs of witchcraft at her house, charms designed to mark her out for death. We also found the mark of the Devil upon her skin.'

'Upon her skin? She's been buried for six weeks!'

'It was deemed advisable to dig her body back up,' Stearne explained, sitting down in our parlour. 'We know the signs, the marks to look for.'

'And of course you found them.'

'"Of course"?' he asked. 'So you are not surprised that they were there, then? What do you know about it?'

'I know nothing,' I replied. 'I just meant that you would find marks whether they were there or not.'

'You're suggesting that I am mistaken?'

'I'm suggesting that you're too keen on your job.'

'It's not a job, my girl,' Stearne said, leaning back and spreading out his legs in the way that men do when they're thinking of matters less holy than this man was pretending to contemplate. 'It's a vocation, a calling. I have given my life to God's work.'

'I don't believe you would know God if he dropped out of the sky and stamped on your foot.'

Stearne's manner changed at that. He leaned forward slightly, by now far too interested in me for my own good.

'You blaspheme easily, girl,' he said. 'You want to watch that tongue of yours – it could get you swinging from a rope.'

Which was when my mother came in. She'd been in the fields nearby, picking wolfsbane and lavender for her medicines. She was a good nurse, my mother, for all her crazy ways (and they're ways that I've learned myself, I'm only too aware of that): she knew how to mix everything from a poultice that would keep a wound fresh to a drink that would relieve pain. She was also a woman who was very good at reading people's thoughts, something she proved that day when she took one look at myself and Stearne and decided, in no time at all, that major trouble was brewing.

'Can I help you?' she asked him.

'This is your daughter?' Stearne asked.

'She is. Why do you ask?'

'I only wonder if it is you that has taught her to take the Lord's business in vain. She has a sinner's mouth.' In fairness Tom the coachman had said similar, though he meant it as a compliment.

'I'm sure,' my mother insisted, 'that whatever she said she meant no disrespect. She's a good girl, though she sometimes opens her mouth without thinking.'

'Clearly,' Stearne replied. 'A shame. And such a beautiful mouth.' He grinned at that and his legs spread a little wider. My mother was by now only too well aware of what was going on – more so than I was at the time.

'I didn't say anything wrong,' I insisted. 'He's the one that misuses the Lord's business, not me.'

'Shush now, Carla,' my mother said. 'Just leave it be.'

Now I can look back on that moment and see that she

was doing her best to shut me up before I made matters so bad that they couldn't be fixed. At the time, though, I had the stupid, rebellious need to argue my point.

'He's a liar,' I said, 'and a dirty pig. You can see what he wants to do with me and it's nothing to do with God!'

Stearne jumped from his seat and ran towards me but my mother was quicker. She grabbed hold of him and held him tight.

'Please, sir,' she said, 'don't hurt her – she doesn't know what she's doing.'

He paused, looking at me. 'Maybe I don't have to look any further for the killer of Old Mother Langley,' he suggested. 'Maybe I've found her.'

'No,' my mother begged. 'Forget about her – she's just a stupid girl, that's all.'

I was about to argue with that when Stearne laughed and pulled my mother close to him. 'I dare say you might be able to convince me,' he said, smiling down at her.

That was it. Looking at him standing there, holding my mother close, I lost my mind to anger. I stormed out of the house and ran right out of the village.

My poor mother. I gave her such a lot to contend with. Not only did she have to bring me up by herself (my father, a lovely gentle soul by all accounts, having died when I was only three) but she had to try and manage my temper too. Look where it got her.

I spent the day walking in the fields above the village, too angry to speak to anyone. Eventually I climbed into one of the old trees that ringed the top of what we called Barnett's Hump (though who Barnett was I have no idea, no doubt he was before my time) and I tried to calm down.

Even at that age I knew that my temper was not helpful. Stearne, however hateful he clearly was, had power and authority. He was a man used to getting what he wanted out of life. All my whining had done was to put both mother and myself in danger.

The best thing to do, I decided, was to go back into the village. Find Stearne and apologise. It would stick in my throat but at least it would keep us safe.

I walked slowly, not looking forward to the task that lay ahead of me. By the time I got to the village it was all over.

'Come now, child,' said Mrs Barrow, the wife of the innkeeper, George Barrow. 'There's nothing for you to see here.'

I wondered what she was talking about. I was momentarily confused about why so many of the villagers were out on the streets and why they all seemed to be staring at me.

'Of course,' said someone in the crowd, 'she's just as bad. Brought up on it, no doubt.'

'Poor thing,' said another. 'Do you think she knew?'

'Knew what?' I asked. Then I said no more as the crowd parted and I saw the body hanging from the tree in the centre of the village.

It was a beautiful spot, with its old cedar and the small pond with its family of ducks. The circle of grass on which I had sat and dreamed away lazy summer afternoons ever since I was a small child. I could never look on it again, not without feeling a chill, not since they hanged my mother there and let her swing for no reason other than the word of a liar. Stearne had exercised his power, all right. Then he had promptly left, along with his master, to go and find new lives to ruin.

'Come on,' said Mrs Barrow again. 'There's nothing to be gained by you looking at it. You just come away.'

Later I realised that she had known that the mood of the crowd was still excitable, that it might not take too much encouragement for them to decide there was more lynching to be done. She was a wise woman, was Mrs Barrow: like all good publicans she knew how to read people.

Of course the enthusiasm for what Hopkins and Stearne had done soon passed, as I imagine it did in most villages. My mother was cut down – I never did find out what happened to the body. She certainly never made it as far as the churchyard – her 'crime' saw to that – and the village made haste to pretend that nothing had happened. I went home and tried to forget, too. I didn't blame the villagers any more than I blamed myself. Maybe that was why it took me as long as it did to do the sensible thing and leave.

And now, a few days later, I am sitting in the barn of a dead man – or at least I hope he is: please let his suffering be over – wondering why my life seems to revolve around those who kill with conviction.

The barn door rattles. When I came in here I drew the bolt because I wanted to be alone.

'Carla?' It's Kronos, come to tell me why he had to do what he's just done. I'm not interested. 'Carla? Let me in. Please.'

No. I don't think so.

I walk over to the coach and run my hand over its lacquered finish. It's a beautiful thing. A pretty box that holds a nasty treasure. I open the door.

It's amazing that it's taken me this long. I think, despite all my concerns, that I didn't want to betray Kronos's trust. He obviously didn't want people looking inside. He blacks out the windows, he keeps the doors closed. Fine, it's private, I understand that. But now . . . now my respect has worn thin and I want to know if there is anything worse to know.

I look inside and think that maybe there is.

It takes me a moment to see in the darkness. All the seats have been removed so that the interior of the coach is just a large box, and in the middle of that box, strapped down to stop it moving, is a coffin.

Why stop now? I ask myself. I could reach for the coffin lid.

'If you had asked,' says Kronos behind me, 'I might have shown you.'

'Might?' I reply, wondering how the hell he got in. Then I remember the hayloft. He probably climbed in through it.

'You assume you have known me long enough that I should share anything with you?'

'No. I suppose not.' I make a grab for the coffin lid, yanking it back so that it clatters against the floor of the coach. The coffin is empty.

'Why have an empty coffin?' I ask. It's just to voice the question really: I don't expect an answer,

Nonetheless Kronos gives me one, unbuttoning his shirt and angling his neck towards the light. There is a scar there. A bite mark. 'It's where I sleep,' he says. Suddenly I realise that I'm in the most terrible danger.

I shove him back and try to run past him. His hand shoots out and snatches at my hair. He keeps some of it but I'm still free. There's a pitchfork leaning against the back wall. I snatch it and turn to face him. I tried to run away from a fight once. It didn't end well and I am determined never to do it again.

'You don't understand,' Kronos says, his teeth clenched. He is angry. And well he might be. But he'll be bloody furious in a minute.

I thrust the prongs of the pitchfork at him, making him tumble to one side rather than be impaled.

'Carla!' he roars. 'You have no idea what you're doing.'

'Never held me back before,' I reply as I follow him and raise the pitchfork. I thrust it forward again and actually catch his side this time. He gives a shout of pain and his shirt tears open to expose a bloody wound.

'I dare say Marcus's wounds were more painful,' I say. 'And you're more of a monster than he ever was.'

'Yes,' Kronos replies, snatching at the pitchfork. 'Much more.'

He manages to yank the implement from my grip and I turn and run, not stupid enough to stay close to him.

Maybe my best hope is to get outside and shout for Grost. Surely he can't be a part of this? Grost is no monster, I'm sure of it, would stake my life on it. *That's exactly what you're doing, my girl,* says my mother's voice in my head.

I make it to the door and my hand is on the bolt when Kronos grabs me from behind and lifts me up into the air. I fight back, swinging my arms and legs, determined that I will not be an easy victim.

'Enough!' he says and throws me across the room where I am lucky enough – at least, I assume it's luck, maybe he just has a good aim – to land in the hay. I am winded but not really hurt.

'I am not a vampire,' he says.

'No,' I reply. 'Of course not. You've been bitten on your neck and you sleep in a coffin but you're not a vampire . . .'

'I fought the infection,' Kronos replies. 'With Grost's help, I fought it and won. The scar remains. And that's good, because it reminds me exactly why I do what I do.'

'So as not to get bitten again?'

'So as not to let others suffer,' he replies. Given what he's done to Marcus this evening, that seems the most absurd thing he's said so far. I tell him so.

Kronos is silent for a moment. He hunches his shoulders and stares at the toes of his boots.

'It was my sister,' he says finally. 'The one who bit me. I had been in Ireland, fighting under Cromwell's orders. I never imagined that my family would be in danger without me.

'As you can tell from my accent I wasn't born in this country. We travelled here when I was small, escaping from Wallachia where my mother and father had been in service to one of the ancient families, that of Lord Varishku, a man so corrupt that he had killed his own brothers to secure the throne. Killed my father, too, though I did not know that until later.

'My mother had taken my sister and me, and we travelled across the country in fear for our lives. From Hungary we made our way to Venice where, she bartered for space on a merchant ship and thus we came here, to England.

'I grew up here, treating this country as my home. I enlisted in its army and I fought its battles. And while I was away . . .

'He was a trader, so he said, from the old country. He met my mother in the market and they got talking of how things had been back home. He was not what he said he was. He infected my mother and sister both. The three of them roamed the area at night to feed.

'When I returned it was to find that a nest of vampires were roosting in my home.

'I killed him easily. His bloodline was susceptible to steel, a problem when you are fighting a man who has a sword.

'Which left my mother and sister. I hesitated.' Kronos points at the wound on his neck. 'As you can tell. But there was nothing left of the people I loved: they were creatures, animals, nothing more.' He pauses, shuffles his feet slightly. 'So I did what had to be done.

'The bite was shallow. And she had not drawn blood. For a vampire to change you, for you to become like them, they have to drink some of your blood and you, in turn, must drink some of theirs. It is an exchange, a contract. I was just poisoned, contaminated as if by the venom in the fangs of a serpent.

'I did not stay in the house. I couldn't bear to be under that roof, not knowing what he had done to them both and what they themselves had gone on to do.

'I walked, heading across the fields and into the night, becoming more and more delirious with every step.

'Grost found me, lying under the stars and howling at the moon, quite out of my mind, He brought me back to myself. He saved my life. And my soul.

'Whatever you may think of what happened to Marcus, he was my friend. I did only what I had to do. He had been turned – nothing can save a man then. In a short time everything that had made him what he was – his personality, his soul – it would all have gone, swallowed by the hunger of the creature he would have become. I could not allow that to happen or I would have been no friend at all.'

I don't say anything. Because I have no idea what to say. Eventually, I speak.

'So why do you sleep in a coffin?'

Kronos hesitates for a little while.

'It makes me think like they do.'

Sometimes men can be so bloody literal.

Forty-Two

Lorrimer's Army

So it comes down to this. Arming ourselves with whatever we can lay our hands on and marching through the village to the doctor's house with vengeance on our mind.

He was a good man, the doctor. I know the others always laughed at me for going on about it but he was. When my Mary was struck down with the plague he didn't hide from her or lock her away like I know lots of doctors did with their patients. He sat with her, risked catching the disease himself, so he did. Rather that than let her be uncomfortable, than let her die in pain.

Like he did himself.

He was just too trusting, that's the beginning and end of it. He couldn't see the darkness men held in 'em. You only have to look at that foreign savage to see there's something wrong, right at the very heart of the man. When he smiles it don't quite reach his eyes, when he laughs the sound has an edge of cruelty, when he acts sincere you can tell he wants something. He is a dark, dark soul. I tried to warn the doctor of that but he wouldn't listen and now he's dead.

There are maybe twenty of us in all, gathered at the White Hart for a drop of courage before we go. Luke Hopkins, Bert Frimpton, Ted Somerton (and he's worth three other men that's for sure), Saul Wilkins, his hefty blacksmith's hammer in his hands . . . all the men what would act.

'We'll have to strike quick,' says Hollis as he pours us all a drink. 'Don't forget I saw him when he killed Kerro and his men. Like lightning he was, barely saw him move.'

'If we all take him at the same instant,' I say, 'crowd him, like, he won't have much of a chance.'

'I've a better idea,' says Luke, holding up a tatty-looking bow. 'I can get him with this from a good step away.'

'With that thing?' I laugh. 'You'll be lucky if you can hit the doctor's house.'

'Kept me and Ma fed for months, this has,' Luke says. 'It may not look up to much but I've a good aim and there's plenty of power in her.'

'All right then,' I say, 'we'll give it a go. You get your shot in and if that don't kill him then we'll be right behind it.'

It's not a long walk and we're outside the doctor's house in no time.

Of course, Luke's found the first problem. 'Where is he?' he asks. 'I can't shoot him if I can't see him.'

'Didn't think of that, did you?' I say, rolling my eyes at him. Of course, I didn't think of it either but there's no point in going on about it.

'He must be asleep,' says Saul. 'If we're quiet maybe

we can sneak up on him – cut his throat before he even has time to open his eyes.'

'No,' says Ted. 'That's not the way this is going to work. I want that bastard to know what's happening. I want him wide awake and scared.'

'Easy for you to say, you big ox,' replies Hollis. 'You didn't see how quick off the mark he is. I say we stove his head in while he's snoring and have done with it.'

'Look,' and now Ted's grabbing Hollis by the scruff of his neck, 'we're not all as cowardly as you. Some of us want to do this honourably.'

'There's no honour in it,' I tell them. 'This is just about putting a dangerous man down before he kills anyone else. Now let's get on with it.'

We move as silently as we can into the courtyard, weapons ready in case the bugger bursts out of the shadows at us.

Luke trips over some of the firewood I chopped earlier. He lands on the cobbles, cursing.

'Brilliant, lad,' I whisper. 'If he didn't already know we were coming he probably does now.'

Kronos has been sleeping in the stables, I know that much. Still, I doubt he'll stay there tonight. Now he's done for the doctor he'll have Marcus's bed, won't he?

I lead everyone to the doctor's front door.

'A couple of you come with me,' I whisper. 'The rest of you stay outside in case he comes sneaking up behind us.'

I test the door. It's not bolted. I open it and me, Luke and Ted walk inside. I'm glad Ted's here: if any of the others stand a chance against the foreigner it's him. I've seen him break men just by squeezing 'em. I notice the axe I use for the firewood and, preferring it to the old sword I'm carrying I give Luke the sword (well, his bow and bloody arrow ain't worked out as much cop, has it?) and I take the axe.

'Unless *you* want it?' I ask Ted.

He shakes his head. 'Better off with just my hands,' he says. And I believe him.

He's a noisy sod on the stairs, though. There's too much of him for the floorboards not to creak when he steps on them.

'Here we are,' I say, pointing ahead to the doctor's bedroom at the top of the stairs.

Ted pushes his way to the front, which is fine by me. As long as we get the job done I don't much care who it is that gets to do it.

We all step into the bedroom and we can tell by the faint light that creeps through the window that Kronos is lying there in bed. We can see the shape of him beneath the sheet.

We all stand there for a minute.

'Well?' I say. 'We going to do this or not?'

I take a deep breath and raise the axe.

'Wait,' says Ted, shoving the body in the bed with his foot. 'I told you I want him awake. I want him to know what's happening, what he's brought down on himself.'

'Fine,' I say. 'So he's awake – nobody sleeps through you kicking 'em a few times.'

I bring the axe down on him, relieved and disgusted in equal measure when I feel it embed itself in his forehead with a solid crunch.

The axe is stuck.

I climb on the bed so that I can get a bit of leverage.

'Luke,' I say, 'how about a bit of light so I can see what I'm doing?'

He strikes his tinderbox and lights a candle. He brings it over to the body and I let out a sob as I realise I've just put my axe into Dr Marcus's corpse.

'Nice work,' says Ted.

'Piss off, Ted Somerton,' I say. 'You were giving him a good kicking earlier, if you cast your mind back.'

It's Luke who asks the only important question. 'Where is he, then?'

Outside there suddenly comes the sound of shouting, cries of pain and the clang of steel against cobbles. The ruckus lasts all of maybe ten seconds and then the night is quiet.

'Oh shit,' I say, wondering exactly how we're going to get out of the trouble we've walked into.

Forty-Three

Brothers in Blood – The Memoirs of Professor
Herbert Grost: Volume One (Unpublished)

Once we had finished, Kronos helped me lift the body of our departed friend upstairs. We laid him out on his bed and I took the opportunity to say a few words.

'He was a God-fearing man,' I said. 'He'd probably want a bit of Bible verse.'

'He didn't fear God,' Kronos said. 'He loved Him. Hopefully, that love was returned.'

He stepped out of the room, leaving me alone with the body. I didn't mind. Sentiment is just another of those things in which I outperform my friend.

I found a Bible next to the bed and read aloud a few of the most cheerful passages I could find. Once done, I pulled the sheet over Marcus's face and left him to his rest.

As I stepped out of the door I spotted something familiar lying on his dresser. Stepping back inside to examine it I realised it was the purse of silver coins.

'Waste not, want not,' I murmured. Then I slipped the coins into my pocket and went downstairs.

As I left the house I became aware of a ruckus coming from inside the stables. It sounded as though Carla and Kronos were fighting. She didn't understand. But that was good: a young soul like her shouldn't have to. I sat down in front of the door and listened as Kronos began to explain to her about his mother and sister.

I'll never forget what he had been like when I found him.

I had been working nearby, tutoring a couple of land-owner's children in a little Latin and Greek. Teaching was by far the most successful way I had found of sustaining myself on the road. I was good at it and, more importantly I think, I looked right. People don't like funny old hunchbacks offering to groom their horses for them or dig a few drainage pits. People that do jobs like that should look young and fit. Teacher? Oh yes . . . you can smell the books on him, that one. Hire him at once! I think it was probably the only time my appearance actually helped me to get work.

I rented a room in a farmhouse at that time, a nice enough little place though the cows woke me up every morning. I was on my way back to it, having stopped off for a little food at the local tavern, when I saw Kronos running wild through one of the fields. The poison hadn't sapped him of his energy, certainly – he was running as if the Devil himself were on his heels. I suppose in many ways he was.

If he had been heading away from me then we would never have met. I couldn't possibly have caught up with him. As it was, he was likely to cut across the road in front of me at any moment so I simply waited.

Then, when he ran directly into a tree on the verge and fell to the ground in a complete faint, I felt it was only my Christian duty to try and nurse him back to consciousness.

It took some time. I managed to convince my farmer landlord that I should be allowed to keep Kronos in my room. (Yes, like a pet dog.) When I explained that, no, I didn't know the gentleman but that I saw it as my duty to try and help him recover, he looked at me as if I were mad.

The first few days were by far the worst. When Kronos was awake he made the fact quite clear by screaming. This did not go down well in the house: my landlord was quite convinced that such a racket would curdle the milk inside the cows.

'Not to mention disease,' he said. 'How do I know that we're not all going to catch what he's got?'

I pointed to the mark on Kronos's neck.

'He was bitten by something,' I explained, 'and poisoned, He's not suffering from the plague or any - thing like that.'

'So *you* say.'

'I can assure you,' I said, 'that however foolish you may think I am, I'm not so foolish as to share a room this size with a plague sufferer. I have no more wish to die than you do.'

In the end I agreed to pay him extra and money succeeded in convincing him where common sense had failed.

Which meant that I had to leave Kronos on his own for a good deal of the day while I continued giving my students their lessons. After all, if I didn't teach I didn't earn and if I didn't earn then that was Kronos and me both out on our ears.

I also spent a little extra time reading in the library of one of my clients. He kept a large selection of books on folklore and witchcraft.

'Old Oliver hasn't much time for this sort of thing,' he joked. 'If the local magistrate knew I had these I'd swing for sure!'

He *was* the local magistrate.

It was the mark on Kronos's neck that made me think of vampires of course. They had fascinated me ever since I was a child and the wound was too suggestive for me to ignore. Unfortunately it seemed almost impossible to get a consensus opinion on what exactly you should do to cure a man who had been bitten. Some said that there was no cure and that the victim would just die slowly. Some said you had to kill the original vampire: doing so would neutralise the supernatural poison present in the bite. Some said that victims were bound to turn into vampires themselves sooner or later and the best thing was to run away very quickly before they did.

Kronos did not turn into a vampire.

In fact, after a few long weeks he began to improve considerably.

'I owe you my life, Grost,' he said one night, 'and I shall never forget it.'

To be fair, he never has.

I pressed my ear to the stable door. It sounded as though Kronos and Carla had finished their arguing for now. Good – we had much more important things to do than bicker among ourselves.

I knocked on the door.

'Well?' I shouted. 'Is somebody going to let me in?'

Carla appeared, an apologetic smile on her face. 'Sorry,' she said. 'I forgot the door was still locked.'

'No, my dear,' I replied. 'It is me who is sorry, sorry for letting you witness the awful incidents of the evening.'

'It's not your fault,' she said. And she was right, it wasn't, but I was nonetheless glad to hear her say so.

Kronos was seated in the open doorway of the coach.

'Oh,' I said. 'Heard all about that, have you?'

'Yes,' Carla replied. 'And if I didn't think Kronos was mad before, I certainly do now.'

'Quite mad.' I accepted her judgement. 'But that may well be an advantage in our line of work.'

'Or an inevitable symptom.'

I nodded, impressed once again by her perspicacity. 'That, too.'

'So now what do we do?' she asked.

'We prepare,' Kronos replied. 'And then we take the fight to the Durwards.'

'You're sure it's them?' Carla asked.

'Who else could it be?' I replied. 'They have the money and the influence.'

'I suppose so,' she agreed, moving over to stand by the window.

'I need to get a fire burning,' I said, 'to melt down those candlesticks.'

'Shush!' hissed Carla, waving her hands at me, still

staring out of the window. 'I just saw someone moving outside.'

Kronos leaped from his seat in the coach doorway and joined her at the window.

'Well?' I asked, with some considerable impatience.

'Looks to be about twenty of them,' he replied, running around and extinguishing the lights. 'Locals – here to lynch us, probably.'

'Oh good,' said Carla. 'My night needed that.'

'Where are you going?' I asked as Kronos jumped towards the hayloft. He just grinned, his big teeth glinting in the moonlight, and pointed upwards.

'Wonderful,' I said, fetching a crossbow from the back of the coach. 'Twenty irate villagers and one smug vampire hunter – how can this not end well?'

I told Carla to stay silent and we both stood to one side of the window, watching the villagers enter the courtyard. Naturally, Clyde Lorrimer was at the front: it was no great surprise to me that he was the ringleader. I also recognised the large man we'd met in the forest, Ted Somerton, the father of poor Freddie Gluckhaven's love, Sally.

He still looked like the sort of man I really wouldn't want to pick a fight with. Yet here I was, picking a fight . . .

Lorrimer, Somerton and one other broke away from the main pack and went inside the house. 'Nothing for you there, gentlemen,' I whispered, watching as the remaining group wandered around nervously, weigh - ing up their weapons and looking startled at every stray noise.

'Where's Kronos?' whispered Carla.

Which was when he jumped off the roof.

Kronos has always enjoyed dramatic entrances. He is also a great believer in being emotionally centred before engaging in battle. I could easily picture him sitting up there, legs crossed, eyes closed, briefly meditating before picking the fattest villager and aiming right for him.

The crowd erupted in panic as one of their number was crushed beneath Kronos's impact.

He drew his swords and spun around, disarming the handful of men who were quick enough to attack after his surprise appearance. It looked as though it was all going to be over in a matter of seconds. They might have the advantage of numbers but they could never hope to match him for skill.

Then one of them struck lucky. The small blacksmith – Saul Wilkins, if memory serves – swung his hammer and let go. It flew towards Kronos and, though he noticed it at the last second and tried to duck, it caught him on the shoulder and brought him down. He was swinging his legs in an arc, lashing out at his attackers as well as trying to get upright again, when their sheer force of numbers pinned him down.

'What are we going to do?' Carla asked as one of the villagers raised a sword to strike.

I kicked open the door to the stables and stepped out, crossbow raised.

'Don't move!' I shouted. 'Or I'll drop you where you stand.'

'Now there's a thing,' came a voice from my left. I

looked to see Lorrimer, Somerton and a third man, one with a drawn bow and an arrow pointed right at me. 'I was just about to say the same.'

Forty-Four

Freddie Gluckhaven Leaves Home

'You coming or not?' Clyde Lorrimer asks me.
'I told you,' I reply. 'I've got nothing against the strangers. They seemed like decent people to me.'

'Decent people?' Lorrimer acts as if I have just named the Lord Himself as a man who is partial to wearing a frock. 'They're cold-blooded killers, that's what they are!'

'So you say,' I reply. 'Far as I can tell the only people who we know for a fact they've killed had it coming. You can't say we'll be sad to see the back of Kerro and his boys.'

'What about Dr Marcus?'

'I'm sorry,' I say. 'You must have been mistaken – they were good friends, the lot of them. There's no way they'd do what you say.'

'Ah, to hell with you, then.' Lorrimer storms off out of the house, away to get his rabble together, his lynch mob. I should do something about it, I know: warn Kronos and his friends. Truth is, though, I find it hard to do much since Sally died.

'When are you going to take the cows in?' mother

asks, shouting from the next room.

I'm not, I think. Let them rot out there for all I care.

'Freddie?' she shouts. 'Answer me, Freddie Gluckhaven. You're not so old that a mother can't give you a lesson with her stick, you know!'

Oh, I think I am, I decide. Plenty old enough, in fact.

'Son?' It's father, holding onto the door frame for support. She's got him so scared that he's come hunting for me. 'Better get on, son,' he says. 'And answer your mother – she's worried about you.'

'She's worried about her cows.'

He shrugs. 'Them, too – they are all we have, you know, Freddie.'

'Yes,' I agree. 'All you have.'

I get up and go to my room. There's a few things I want to collect: a chain of Sally's, a couple of letters she wrote to me, things to remember her by.

'Freddie!' Mother is roaring now, her voice harsh and distorted as she tightens up her throat to fling her anger even further. 'Freddie, I know you can hear me! You just get yourself in here where I can see you!'

No, I think. No goodbyes.

I step out of the front door and walk away from the house, the sound of mother's screaming following me all the way into the dark of the forest.

I don't know where I'm going. But it'll be anywhere but here.

Forty-Five

Carla Takes a Bite

What can we do? Kronos is held down, a sword point about to pierce his throat. If Grost shoots the man holding that sword then he'll have an arrow in his head before his bolt has even found its mark. We are trapped, none of us wanting to make a move first.

Well, except me, of course. Nobody's ever been able to make me behave.

'Stop this,' I shout, stepping out into the courtyard. 'A good man has died tonight and now you want to kill one more?'

'I see no good man,' sneers Lorrimer.

I walk up to him, hands on my hips. 'For once, Clyde Lorrimer, I quite agree with you!'

That's him told.

'You're all attacking the wrong people,' I shout. 'The real enemies here are the Durwards. They are not what they appear, and unless you let us go they'll destroy everyone in this village one by one.'

'Don't give me that,' says Lorrimer. 'You'll say anything to save your skin.'

Suddenly there is a groan from behind me and I turn

to see a man bring his sword down on the man threatening Kronos. The sword takes his arm off above the elbow and the impasse is broken.

'Get away from him!' shouts Luke Hawkins, turning his aim towards the new aggressor. Grost takes the opportunity as soon as it's offered, changing his aim and shooting Luke before he can loose his own arrow. As Luke is hit, the arrow goes wild, hitting someone in the crowd.

Kronos is on his feet, both swords back in his hands as he spins and roars in a mixture of rage and pleasure.

Lorrimer charges forward with his axe but Somerton grabs it from him and claims it for his own.

'You killed my Sally!' he shouts and runs at Kronos.

'No,' says the helpful new stranger as he skips out of the way and strikes his sword against Somerton's legs. The big man falls and the stranger is quick to kick the axe to one side. 'Consider yourself lucky,' he says, reversing his sword and swinging the hilt down so that it whacks Somerton right in the head. The big man is out for the count.

And what do I do? You might well ask . . .

'Lorrimer!' I shout and jump on the panicking little pig as he tries to run away. 'Lend me your ears!' I ask him, leaning down to sink in my teeth.

Lorrimer screams and I let him run.

When I turn back I see that most of the villagers are chasing after him, bar the few that will be running nowhere anytime soon.

'So,' says the stranger, whose name turns out to be Freddie Gluckhaven. 'You say it's the Durwards that killed my Sally? Tell me more . . .'

Forty-Six

Barton Sorrell Falls Again

Will I ever stop falling? I thought I'd hit the ground a long time ago when I lay there, eyes watering from the brightness of the sun and the pain in my shattered legs. Then I began to doubt, when I held Ann, sobbing, in my arms. Then again when I held her for the last time. Surely now, I thought, gazing on the cold, dead face of my beloved sister, surely now I have finally fallen as far as any man can possibly fall.

But maybe not.

Pa is sitting on the porch, staring at the stars and smoking his pipe, Sometimes he forgets to light it, then I do it for him and he carries on, occasionally puffing out small clouds to float up and obscure the moon.

Isabella is finding it harder to cope than she would ever admit. Between my anger and Pa's emptiness, she just doesn't know what to do with herself. Of course, I could try and help, could stop raging at everything that comes into reach. I could do that.

But I wish it would all just burn. I honestly think that's the only thing that would please me now, to watch it *all* burn.

The coach comes rattling up the track before stopping outside the house.

'Is that the Durwards?' I wonder. 'What do they want?'

Then I see what steps out and walks slowly up to the front porch.

Pa doesn't see it properly for a moment, just stares at it without thinking. Then he notices and the screaming brings my sister running.

'Oh, dear God,' she says, as it raises one hand to tear out Pa's throat. The hand knocks the lantern swinging from the corner of the porch and the orange light sweeps backwards and forwards so that the sight of Pa being torn apart steps in and out of shadow. 'What is it?' she screams as she runs back into the house to find something to fight with.

'That, dear sister,' I say, 'is what's going to tear a hole in the guts of the world itself.'

She doesn't appear as pleased about it as me. But then, Isabella always was the awkward one.

'Yes,' I say, eagerly dropping to my knees and breathing deep of the steam that comes from my dead father's carcass. 'Let's fall together!'

Forty-Seven

Brothers in Blood – The Memoirs of Professor Herbert Grost: Volume One (Unpublished)

We told young Freddie Gluckhaven all we knew and much of what we suspected.

He was a changed man since last we'd seen him. He carried with him a sense of determination and . . . was it detachment? Yes . . . I rather think it was. The frothing emotion of before had boiled away, leaving a man who had decided what he must do and who would not be stopped from doing it.

Dear God, but he reminded me of Kronos.

'So we must take the fight to the Durwards,' he said.

'Indeed,' I replied. 'But we have a great deal to prepare first.'

'What's to prepare?' he asked. 'We know who the enemy is, we have a sword in our hand, so let's get on with it.'

'Your sword will do you no good,' said Kronos. 'Have you not been listening? Every vampire bloodline has a different weakness. These creatures are killed by silver.'

'Both of them?' Freddie asked.

'They may have different feeding habits,' I explained. 'One feeds on youth, the other simply kills in a frenzy. But silver will kill them both.'

'So,' Freddie said, 'Paul and Sara Durward . . . I'm surprised . . . well, no, I can believe anything of Sara but Paul always seemed . . . I don't know: cold, but decent enough.'

'I've been thinking about that,' I said, 'bearing in mind everything that Marcus told us about both of them. Paul Durward is a quiet, repressed individual, someone who has always been held back and pushed down by others.'

'You think this lunatic that's tearing people apart is his animal side?' Carla asked.

'It's possible,' Kronos agreed. 'He may not even know what he becomes . . . a creature of pure instinct let loose!'

'Not for long,' said Freddie. 'We'll see to that. So when do we attack?'

'Tomorrow,' said Kronos. 'We shall tear that family—'

There was a terrible scream from somewhere out in the woods.

'Quickly!' Kronos shouted. He jumped to his feet and ran into the darkness.

I went to the stables, strapped a saddle on our fastest horse and chased after him.

I followed the sound of screaming as well as the occasional glimpses of Kronos in the moonlight. It was the Sorrell household, I realised as we drew close. Marcus had said that they lived close-by.

There was a soft noise, like a sheet whipping in the wind, and then the forest was lit by a blaze of fire.

'Kronos!' I shouted, coming alongside him so he could climb up and take the reins.

We rode towards the Sorrell's home, unable to miss it now that it was a fireball in the middle of the forest.

'They've been here!' said Kronos, leaping off the horse as we came to the front of the small house.

He scanned the ground, noting the tracks left by a coach as it had sped away from the scene of destruction.

'Dear Lord,' I said, looking down on what must have been the remains of George Sorrell. He had been torn apart. 'That's not just the result of the coach running over him, surely,' I said.

Kronos squatted down to examine the body. 'No, he was attacked, as if by an animal. This last . . .' he pointed to where the man's right arm had been severed '. . . is where the coach ran over him. But the rest was done by hand.'

'By hand?'

'This creature is incredibly strong, my friend,' said Kronos. 'You can see where the skin and muscle was torn – that's no weapon, that's teeth and nails.'

I stared into the heat of the fire. 'Poor family,' I said. 'They got them all in the end.' I could just see what was left of the brother and sister. The boy was propped up in the corner of the porch, what looked like the remains of a crutch sticking up from the top of his head like the antenna of an insect. The girl was hanging from the far end of the roof: the flames had caught her clothes and she had burned like a foul candle. The shadow of her cremated bones was showing through the flames.

'Don't worry, my friend,' said Kronos. 'This will be the end of it. Nobody else dies now except the foul creatures that did this. Tomorrow we finish this business once and for all.'

Forty-Eight

Carla Is Not Patient

I'm not good at waiting. Never have been. If I know that something needs doing then I'm the sort of person that just has to get on and do it (or hide and pretend it didn't really need doing – you know, if it's one of those things that you're supposed to do but *really don't want to*).

This business of waiting a whole day before we attack the Durwards, well . . . By mid-morning I'm nearly out of my mind. Freddie's not much better.

'Surely it would make more sense to attack during the day?' he asks Grost. 'Aren't vampires scared of sunlight?'

'They're not scared of anything,' he replies. 'And as we will be fighting them inside it really doesn't matter a great deal, does it? "Excuse me," ' he joked, ' "would you mind awfully coming over here to the window while we're duelling?" '

'There's no need for sarcasm,' says Freddie and heads off outside for a sulk.

I decide to stay and watch Grost for a while. It's fascinating to see him go about the business of melting down the candlesticks, puffing the bellows to build the flames higher and higher.

'You could have been a smith,' I tell him.

'I've done most jobs in my time,' he admits. 'The worst, by far, was nursemaiding, the best was probably when I worked as a food tester.'

'Food tester?'

'For a mad old earl who was convinced that his cook was trying to poison him. He wasn't, of course – I mean these are civilised times! Still, there was no convincing him so I had to eat a portion of everything he did. I put on a great deal of weight and lived a happy life.'

'What went wrong?'

'I fell out with the cook.'

'So?'

'Well . . . I thought he might try to poison me.'

'Silly man.'

Once the candlesticks are melted, Grost tips the liquid metal into a mould. 'Right,' he says, 'that's that for a while. Let's busy ourselves with other matters.'

'Other matters?'

'Indeed! I won't have Kronos going into battle with - out first making sure that I have taken care of every possible eventuality.'

'Such as?' Grost can be hard work when he wants to be.

'I was thinking of how the vampire that feeds on youth ensnared its victims. Marcus described Ann Sorrell being left in a daze. Some vampires possess a kind of mesmerism, an ability to freeze you in your tracks. All they have to do is make eye contact with you.'

'Right – so don't look at their eyes.'

'Easier said than done,' Grost replies. 'I have something better in mind.' He taps the surface of Marcus's mirror. 'Now all I have to do is find a big enough diamond to cut it.'

'Well, when you've finished with it . . .'

'It's yours, my dear!'

I leave him muttering away to himself and rifling through drawers.

I wonder what Kronos is up to?

When I step outside Freddie soon tells me. 'He's on the roof,' he says. 'Asleep, by the looks of him.'

'He's meditating,' I explain.

'Oh yes?' What's that then?'

'I think it's a bit like sleeping.'

Freddie gives a polite chuckle, then wanders towards the front entrance.'They won't stay away for ever you know,' he says.

'Who?'

'The folk from the village. Sooner or later they'll be back.'

'As long as they wait until nightfall,' I reply. 'By then we'll be gone.'

'And then?'

I shrug. 'Then gone somewhere else, I suppose.'

'Is that all you do? Travel from place to place, killing monsters?'

'It's all *they* do,' I say. 'I'm new at it and I can't see me continuing.'

'Oh, I thought you and Kronos were . . .'

'There is no room in Kronos's life for anyone but

himself,' I explain, not unkindly. 'He is not someone who you could share a life with.'

'And you've had enough vampires to last you for a while?'

'More than enough,' I say. 'But it's not fear or anything like that. I wouldn't want to become the kind of person that a life like this makes you into, that's all.'

Freddie nods at that but I'm not sure he really understands. I hope he does soon. I wouldn't want Freddie Gluckhaven to become that sort of person either. Right now a large shadow hangs over him and nobody could blame him for wanting revenge. Once this business is over, though, he needs to try and forget; people who cling to the past have no life at all – that's something I know well enough.

We eat lunch together, accepting that Kronos and Grost should be left alone to get on with whatever preparations they feel the need to make. They know their business and all we would do is distract them.

It is hard to make small talk with a man who carries such grief.

Freddie wanted to know my plans for my life after this. I ask him the same question. If nothing else it makes us feel it's more likely that we will survive the coming battle.

'I have no idea,' he admits. 'I just can't stay here any more. I've got a small bag of belongings and a strong urge to keep walking, that'll see me clear for now.'

'Plans only get in the way of opportunities,' I tell him.

'True enough,' he agrees. 'I would have left years ago but . . .'

'Sally,' I say.

He nods.

'Well, it took me years to finally get up the courage,' I admit, 'and the locals really did work hard to encourage me. First stop: here and certain death.'

'Maybe you should have turned left, not right.'

We laugh a little. Freddie is happy to be distracted from his thoughts and I am happy to distract him. He is good company.

Finally, as the afternoon moves towards evening, Grost comes and finds us.

'Come on, then, you two,' he says. 'You can't hang around here all day. We have vampires to kill!'

Forty-Nine

Brothers in Blood – The Memoirs of Professor Herbert Grost: Volume One (Unpublished)

A nd so, to the plan!
Storming Durward Hall really was not an
option. Quite simply, four people cannot really 'storm'
anything. So we decided to employ a modicum of
cunning. Carla and Freddie would approach from the
front, making themselves known to the household and,
if possible, keeping the Durwards distracted for long
enough for Kronos and I to gain access from one of the
windows above.

Carla and Freddie would make it clear that they were
visiting with the full knowledge of friends and family in
the village. That should, we hoped, be enough to stop
the Durwards simply killing the pair of them the minute
they uncorked the sherry.

'"Should,"' said Freddie. 'What a useless word.'

'Yes,' I admitted. 'But the most appropriate one right
now, I'm afraid.'

'We'll be all right,' said Carla. 'If they get funny you
can poke your crucifix at them.'

I had decided to give the silver crucifix to Freddie

so that he wouldn't be completely unarmed.

'You won't be alone with them for long,' Kronos reassured them. 'Just keep them distracted while we gain entrance above. We'll have them trapped in the middle. Then,' he clapped his hands, 'we close our trap.'

As plans go it was certainly not our most refined. Still, it was at least an improvement on our last hunt and the execution of Madam Loubrette. Kronos's plan then had been 'We go in, kill everyone, then get on the road by lunchtime so that we're home before dark.'

Kronos was not a man who liked to plan things to death.

The time had come for our final preparations. I had told Carla earlier that I liked to deal with every possible eventuality before allowing Kronos into battle. Now I extended that to all of us. There had been too many deaths already – including that of poor Marcus. Of course, I couldn't guarantee that any of us would escape Durward Hall with our lives but I would at least do everything in my power to increase our chances.

'This,' I announced, placing a small phial on the table, 'is an infusion of garlic and wolfsbane. It smells terrible but I nonetheless insist that we all smear some on ourselves.'

'It does no good,' moaned Kronos, as he always did. 'It just makes your eyes water for five minutes until it dries.'

'Nonetheless,' I insisted, 'you will apply some, with particular attention to the neck.'

Soon the room was pungent with the smell of garlic.

'"Oh, hello, Mrs Durward,"' joked Carla. '"I just wondered if Freddie and I could come in and use your bath."'

'The smell wears off once it's dry,' I promised them. 'You won't draw attention to yourselves.'

Next came the blood candle.

I had purchased the soft red stumps from a Catholic who claimed they had provenance from the Vatican itself. Simply owning it would be more than enough to get you hanged as a papist. It was a combination of wax, holy water and the blood of a saint. Where they get saint's blood from I have no idea but the man owed me money and I took them in lieu.

I used the soft wax to daub the sign of the cross on the napes of Kronos's and Carla's necks. Freddie wore his hair short so it was a little more difficult in his case. I certainly didn't want it to show. In the end we decided his collarbone was as close as we could get and if the candles were of any worth at all it should be close enough.

I had already given Freddie my cross, so that he and Carla had something silver with which to defend them - selves, I ensured each of the rest of us had a smaller, simpler crucifix too. Their efficacy is mixed (I have the impression that it all rather depends on how religious the vampire is) but it did us no harm whatsoever to carry them.

Finally I unveiled the sword. I had done a good job on it, even if I do say so myself. (And if I don't nobody will: Kronos is not one for compliments.)

'The blade is pure silver,' I said, 'manufactured from

the candlesticks plus the silver coins that the Durwards spent on their assassin.'

'Nice touch,' said Carla.

'I thought so. They can have their money back, eh, Kronos?'

He held the sword in his hand, testing its weight. 'It feels good,' he admitted.

That was as close as I would ever get to: 'Grost, you have made a very nice sword.' I don't mind. I know he thought it – that was the important thing.

'It feels good from that end,' I told him. 'Let us hope that the same cannot be said from the other.'

I held up the small device I had constructed by using the mirror from Marcus's bedroom. 'Here is a little addition.'

It was a piece of mirror affixed to a metal sleeve so that it fitted snugly onto the blade of the sword. Kronos looked at it, smiled and then held up the sword so the mirror covered his eyes but captured the reflection of my own.

'To ward off their mesmerism, eh, Grost?' he asked.

'That was rather the idea. In a perfect world they will become transfixed themselves as long as you hold their reflection in the glass.'

'A perfect world?' asked Carla. 'Since when have we lived in one of those?'

'Every vampire we kill,' I replied, 'takes us one step closer.'

Fifty

Carla Meets the Durwards

'Are you ready?' I ask Freddie.

'Am I not supposed to be asking you that?' He smiles. 'Not much seems to scare you.'

'Where does fear get you?'

'Somewhere safe?'

'No, that's common sense. But then, I've never had much of that, either . . .'

We walk up the drive of Durward Hall, a grim-looking building that I imagine looks no more wel-coming during daylight.

'Look at the size of the place,' I say. 'They must get lost in it.'

'So much house for so few people,' Freddie agrees, 'when there are those with no home at all.'

'Well, I shouldn't let that trouble you too much. In an hour's time it'll be empty – there'll be no more Durwards living in it.'

'Good,' Freddie replies and there is a look that passes across his face that almost breaks my heart.

'You loved her very much, didn't you?' I ask him.

He nods. 'More than I can say. I am so much less

without her. And all because some foul creature wanted to look young. It could have been anyone – she meant nothing to them.'

'And everything to you.'

'Yes.'

I take his hand. 'It won't bring her back, but at least we can make sure it doesn't happen to anyone else.'

We reach the entrance porch. It's as big as my mother's cottage but with a lot more pillars.

I ring the doorbell. Then again. Then once more.

'It is a big house,' says Freddie. 'Maybe they can't find the front door.'

As he speaks it opens and we are greeted by Paul Durward himself.

'My apologies,' he says. 'The butler seems to have vanished.'

'How remiss of him,' I say, offering a curtsy.

'How can I help you?' Durward asks, clearly not willing to let us in without a good reason.

'Well, sir,' says Freddie, digging up the rehearsed story, 'it's like this. You may not have heard but the local church is having some work done on it and we were wondering if you had any objection to our naming a window after you?'

'A window?'

'Yes, sir.'

'Named after me?'

'Well, after the Durward family, sir, not just you in particular.'

Paul Durward stares at us for a short while, clearly thrown by the suggestion.

'Why on earth would you want to do a thing like that?'

Oh, let us in, you miserable sod! I think. We just offered to name a bit of stained glass after you – don't be so ungrateful.

'Well, sir,' I say, 'it's like . . . it's like . . .' And I promptly fall over.

This throws Freddie because it's unplanned. But then, the window idea still has us stuck on the doorstep and I do so like to be spontaneous.

'Carla!' he cries, dropping down next to me.

'What on earth's wrong with the girl?' asks Durward.

'Haven't a bloody clue,' Freddie whispers so softly that only I can hear him. 'Some illness of the brain, I imagine.' Louder he says: 'She's just come over faint, I think, sir, I don't suppose we could . . . that is to say, just for a moment . . . ?'

'Oh,' Paul Durward sighs, 'bring her in.'

He steps back and Freddie lifts me up – rather roughly, actually.

'You're too kind, sir,' he says. 'Really, I'm sure she'll be all right if she can just get her breath back for a moment.'

Paul Durward leads us through into the massive drawing room where a log fire is crackling away.

'I'll just place her here,' says Freddie, 'in front of the fire.'

'As you like,' says Paul Durward.

'What's the problem, dearest?' a woman's voice asks and, opening one eye, I see Sara Durward enter the room. She is wearing an almost exact copy of her brother's clothes: tight britches, a florid ruff, velvet jacket. A fine-looking pair, I think, before giving a solid, theatrical groan and writhing on the *chaise longue* like a creature afflicted.

'They're from the church, sister,' says Paul, 'or something like that. Unfortunately, one of them has had a bad turn.'

'The church?' Sara laughs. 'What on earth would anyone from the church want here?'

'To name a window after us, apparently.'

'A window?' Sara laughs again. 'Darling, you're being quite ridiculous.'

Paul shrugs and gestures towards us. 'I'm only repeating what they said.'

Sara walks over to us and I decide it's time to feel better. At least that way I can help Freddie with the explanations.'

'Madam,' Freddie bows towards her, 'my apologies for this embarrassing situation. I'm sure Carla will be feeling more herself any moment now.'

'Yes,' says Sara, 'I'm sure she will. What's this non - sense about a church window?'

'As I explained to your brother, madam, we are conducting extensive work on the church, including the placement of a new window. We wanted the window to be dedicated to the Durward family, as a sign of respect.'

'Respect? What earthly respect for the Durwards would be felt by the people of Padbury? We've barely set foot in the place for years.'

'Nonetheless . . .'

I give another short groan and then sit up straight. 'I don't know what came over me,' I announce. 'Most strange . . . I'm sure I'm on the mend now. Perhaps – oh, I presume too much – a small brandy?'

Sara laughs. 'The good little Christian wants a brandy.'

'Purely for its medical benefits, you understand,' I reply. 'Otherwise I'd never touch the stuff.'

Paul sighs. 'Where the hell is the brandy?' He starts wandering around the room on the hunt for a decanter.

'I don't suppose you've been in service, have you?' Sara asks Freddie, with a sly grin. 'We could do with a new butler.'

'Sadly, no, madam,' he replies, until I give him a surreptitious kick on the ankle. 'Though I dare say I could turn my hand to most things.'

'Butler, footman, charlady . . .' Paul sighs again, having given up on finding the brandy. 'In the last week we've been shedding servants like a drowning dog loses fleas.'

'What a lovely simile, dear,' says his sister, rolling her eyes.

'Hmm? Oh, sorry . . .' Paul pours a glass of sherry and hands it to me. 'You'll have to make do with sherry, I'm afraid, I can't find anything else.'

'Sherry's lovely, thank you,' I reply, before remembering my Puritan manners. 'Probably.'

I take a sip and watch the two Durwards. Sara certainly fits the description of the vampire: she is young and beautiful, though it is an unconventional sort of beauty – she has those looks that a person can have when you're not quite sure whether you think they're funny-looking or gorgeous. Perhaps it's the men's clothes she wears . . . a strange affectation, certainly. As for Paul, his manner is harmless enough – but who knows what animal aspects might be released should he undergo any change into a monstrous other self?

Drink your sherry quickly and get out! says a voice in my head – my mother's voice, in fact, the one that's always trying to keep me out of trouble. Sorry, mother, but I think I'll have to stay a little longer. I have a job to do, you see. I wonder how Kronos is doing: has he got inside yet? Could he be on his way downstairs this very minute?

'So,' says Sara, 'what do you really want?'

I nearly choke on my sherry. 'I'm sorry?'

'Only what we said,' insists Freddie. 'They asked us to come up here and get your permission, maybe even discuss a few designs.'

'"They"?' asked Sara – and I was pleased that Freddie had managed to drop in the suggestion that others knew where we were. It was something I had quite forgotten.

'Ah, well, the village council, you know, the people who thought it might be an nice idea in the first place.'

'Village council? There's only about twelve people living there – it hardly warrants a council.'

'How else do you get things done?' Freddie asks. 'You've got to have a council.'

This is all getting far too complicated for its own good.

'It doesn't matter, sister,' says Paul. 'If they want to name a window after us, then let them.' He looks to me. 'Now, if you're feeling better?'

Oh dear, I think they're going to get rid of us.

'Well, actually . . .' What to say? What to say? 'We were rather hoping you might offer a donation.'

'I knew it!' laughs Sara. 'There had to be a reason for it – they want our money!'

Now, I thought, either I've just bought us some more time or we'll be thrown out within seconds. As it happened, neither alternative is correct.

There is the sound of breaking glass from above. Both Paul and Sara leap to their feet.

'What the devil?' Paul dashes to the window in time to see the remains of an upstairs window rain down onto the drive. 'Mother?' he asks.

Sara gives both of us a particularly vicious look. 'Watch them!' she says and runs out of the room.

Paul looks confused, torn between his desire to do as his sister tells him and also to see what the trouble is upstairs.

'Don't let us detain you,' Freddie suggests, glancing over Paul's shoulder at the window behind him. 'Oh God . . . is that Sara?'

Paul, not the brightest boy in the room, turns around to look. Freddie hits him over the head with a sizeable vase of marigolds.

'Well done!' I say, jumping over to check on the soaked and flower-bedecked nobleman. 'Who needs silver when you've got decorative flowers?'

'Eh?' Freddie is confused for a moment, then the

penny drops. 'I see what you mean . . . do you think maybe he's not . . . ?'

We run into the entrance hall. A door on the other side suddenly bursts open in a shower of splinters and a fractured bolt. Beyond it there seems to be nothing but darkness. Then, slowly, a figure appears. It is hunched and naked, its skin covered in blisters and warts and stained dark by earth. Great patches of hair are missing from its head, leaving those few that have continued to grow to hang long, dangling past its cruel, misshapen face. It looks at us and howls, revealing a mouth of irregular teeth.

'What in God's name is it?' shouts Freddie.

'Ah,' says a woman's voice from the stairs. She is beautiful, a little older than me, perhaps, but I will think myself lucky to age with such grace. Her long red hair shines in the candlelight and as her stare falls on me I realise that I cannot move. Oh no . . . Grost warned me of this . . . the mesmerism of a vampire . . . 'I am Lady Durward,' she announces, stepping fully into the room, 'I see you've met my husband.' She gestures towards the creature in the other doorway. 'Hagen,' she con - tinues, 'come and greet our guests.'

Fifty-One

Kronos

Always the battle awaits. Always one more creature to put to the sword, or the stake, or the flame. Always there is one more fight to win.

It has been so long this way that I am not sure I would want it any other.

This is who I am: a man who kills vampires. It is the very essence of me. And I am proud.

Grost and I watch Carla and Gluckhaven walk to the front door of Durward Hall. They stand there for some time, Carla ringing the bell, Freddie twitching nervously. He is a good man, this Freddie Gluckhaven, but he is not a warrior. Not yet.

Finally the door opens and I catch my first glimpse of Paul Durward. I am disappointed: he is not the strong and noble-looking man I might have hoped for. He does not look like his father's son. I remember Hagen on the field of battle – he was a man who becomes an extension of his worst tendencies. He was a man who killed. His muscles all pulled in that direction, and directed his sword to his every nuanced command. He was a physical man.

This man is not physical. This is a body whose only purpose is to convey the soul inside it from one whimsy to another. His hair is light blond, curly like a girl's. His skin is soft and pale, like spilled milk.

'He is not our man,' I tell Grost.

'Who is to say what changes come over him when he is transformed?' Grost replies.

'No. He is nothing – trust me.'

Grost shrugs. 'If you say so. But that means we're hunting for someone else in the house. A servant, perhaps?'

'Perhaps. Let's find out.'

Gluckhaven and Carla finally step inside and Grost and I run across the lawns to the side of the house. A sizeable growth of ivy clings to the wall: it has been allowed to grow too thick, threatening to consume half the house. It will make the climb easy.

'Ah,' says Grost. 'Ivy, friend to vampire hunters, burglars and illicit lovers.'

'Just climb,' I tell him.

The house is ostentatious and built in the European style. Each window has its own balcony, which makes things much easier for us. This is just as well: Grost is a good man but physical exercise is not his strength. He is out of breath by the time we climb over the balustrade and down onto one of the first-floor balconies.

'We can use the stairs to leave, yes?' he asks.

'Enter with stealth, leave with confidence,' I assure him. 'Or not at all.'

'Yes, he replies. 'Thank you for reminding me of that possibility.'

265

He has brought his beloved crossbow and he holds it in front of him now as I force open the window. The crossbow is perfect for Grost: the only thing you really need in order to kill someone with it is a good eye. Thanks to his spectacles, Grost has this. He can take a difficult shot and make it count. Of course, it's no use at all in close combat. But then, if Grost ends up in that position he's already dead.

The room we enter is dark and I motion for Grost to stay absolutely still while our eyes get used to the dim light from the open window. I listen, aware of the sound of breathing. Typical – a house this size shared by three people and we break into an occupied room. We have seen Paul Durward downstairs so it cannot be him. I think it unlikely that Sara would be lying up here in the dark, either. So it is the mother, the woman who 'suffers from grief'. I cannot afford to let her sound the alarm so I send Grost to one side of the bed with his tinderbox while I take the other. On a count of three, he strikes a light while my hand clamps down on the mouth of the person in the bed.

It is not Lady Durward.

The man is old, though who knows if it is his natural age? He is badly wounded. Blood trickles from a cut on his forehead, another in his throat. His eyes open and meet mine but he is not afraid. I am not the worst thing that could happen to him: he has already endured that.

He is naked and, as Grost lifts the light, I can see that his entire body is covered in cuts and bruises. Occasional sparkles reveal themselves to be the jewelled heads of hatpins, inserted through his flesh at random.

'Dear God,' says Grost. 'What's happened to this man?'

'He has been tortured,' I reply. 'Slowly and heartlessly.'

The man tries to speak. I am sure that he is not our enemy.

'Where is she?' he asks. 'Have you seen her?'

'Who?' asks Grost. 'Sara Durward?'

The man looks confused, then slowly shakes his head. 'No, Lady Durward, not Sara . . . where is she?'

'We do not know,' I tell him. 'We have only just arrived. Is she in trouble?'

He actually laughs at that, though the panic in his eyes robs all the humour from the sound. 'Nobody could harm Lady Durward,' he says. 'She's the one who did this to me . . . nobody knows how . . .' He begins to cough and I consider placing the pillow over his face. I sympathise with his pain but I do not want to draw attention to our presence. As he coughs, one of the wounds in his side, just below the ribs, begins to bleed and I take the light from Grost to investigate. The blood is thin and the sheet below him is already soaked with it. The man has not long to live, I'm sure.

Finally he gets the coughing under control.

'Tell Nell,' he says. 'Tell Nell I died better than this.'

Then he is silent. Grost shakes his head. 'Nell?'

'A wife?' I shrug. 'A lover? It doesn't matter. He is just another victim whom we need to avenge.'

Grost lights the candles by the bedside and we explore the room. A small door leads off it into a dressing room.

'So Lady Durward is not what she appears,' says Grost.

'Most definitely not.' I draw his attention to the wig stand on the dressing table. Over it is draped what appears to be a human face, aged and wrinkled.

Grost picks it up and a cloud of perfumed wig powder is released from beneath it. It doesn't quite mask the smell of decay.

'Oh Lord,' he says, flinging it to the table where it slaps against the varnished wood. 'It's real. Not a mask – it's an actual human face.'

'What better disguise?' I ask him as I walk towards the door that leads onto the corridor.

'What better, indeed?' says a female voice. Lady Durward erupts from the shadows of the dressing room, pushing me back towards the window. If I could have doubted her vampiric heritage earlier she would have assured me now: her strength is far greater than a man's.

I curse myself for my ineptitude as I hit the window and feel it give way behind me.

I am surrounded by the sound of breaking glass and splintering wood, spinning blades of it catching the moonlight and sparkling as I fall back against the balus - trade, my balance tipping me over and into the open air.

The ivy! I think. *Friend to vampire hunters, burglars and illicit lovers.* My hands snatch for it and I manage to grab hold of a branch before following the remains of the window onto the driveway below.

'Grost!' I shout as I hear him cry out above me. If my stupidity has killed him I swear there will not be enough vampire blood in the world to wash the memory of it clean.

I'm hanging backwards by only one hand, and I'm damned if I'm dropping my sword in order to get a better grip. I put the blade between my teeth and throw myself forward so that I can grab the ivy with both hands. More secure now, I start to climb back up, moving as quickly as I can and hoping that Grost has managed to stay alive in the meantime.

I needn't have worried.

'Want a hand?' he asks, reaching down over the balustrade.

'Don't tell me you managed to kill her?' I ask, frankly shocked.

'Don't be silly,' Grost replies. 'She threw me through a vanity mirror and then strolled off. I have a feeling I have been underestimated.'

'As usual.' I take his hand and climb back inside the dressing room.

From downstairs, there is the sound of splintering wood before an inhuman roar echoes up towards us.

'I rather think Carla and Freddie may need our help,' says Grost.

We run from the room and onto the landing. The sounds from below grow louder: a woman screams – not Carla, I realise, she is not the sort to scream easily – and a man shouts before there is the sound of more wood splitting.

'Quickly, Kronos!' Grost shouts, running for the stairs.

As if I need the encouragement.

Arriving at the stairway, we can see down into the entrance hall and our players are revealed.

Gluckhaven is in the entrance hall, Carla at his side. In his hands he is holding a tall wrought-iron candelabrum. He is using this to keep back the creature that is pursuing them. At first glance I could mistake it for an animal: it's hunched over as if it's ready to run on all fours, its skin is dark and covered in blisters. Then I shout and it looks up towards me. I recognise its face. Hagen Durward, once death and the plague has had its way with him.

'It's her husband,' I tell Grost. 'She has brought him back to life.'

'Reanimation?' Grost says. 'Which is why she was so hungry for the life force of others – she was channelling it into him!'

'Looks good on it, too,' I remark.

The woman in question is walking a few steps behind what is left of her husband, offering him gentle words of encouragement: soft, adoring noises. She sounds as though she's talking to a dog.

'Father?' Sara Durward is huddled in a corner, her hands pressed against her mouth, clearly terrified. Her brother just stands and stares at the creature that sired him.

When it hears her voice, the creature turns its head towards her and makes a gurgling noise.

'Hagen,' says Lady Durward, 'do concentrate, my love. You can play with the children later.'

But Hagen is not to be dissuaded. He lopes towards the girl, stretching himself upwards and extending his arms, whether to embrace or attack her it is impossible to tell.

'No!' Paul Durward shouts, finding courage at last. He jumps on his father's back and tries to wrestle him to the ground. He doesn't even begin to provide a contest. Hagen flings him back so that he slides across the floor tiles and hits the wall.

He buys me a little time, though, and that is appreciated.

Grost often tells me off for making dramatic entrances. He says that I like showing off too much. I would argue that swinging from the chandelier is quicker than taking the stairs. It also gives me enough momentum to kick Hagen halfway across the entrance hall, though my thigh muscles will not thank me later for doing so.

He is quick to get to his feet and he charges back towards me. Gluckhaven catches him first, stabbing him with the tip of the candelabrum and opening a wound in the creature's side.

'Leave him to me!' I insist. 'Look to the wife!'

He turns to do so but Lady Durward has already began to use her magic.

'Don't look into her eyes!' I hear Grost shout.

I cannot concern myself with both of them for now. Let them fight the woman – Hagen is *mine*.

Despite the glutinous jelly leaking from his side, he seems unaffected by Gluckhaven's attack. He wipes at the oozing purple gloop with one of his pink-raw hands and holds it to his nose. Reanimation is clearly not a perfect science. I can see little of Hagen Durward in this

271

animal. But then, as he gives another doglike roar and runs towards me I realise that maybe this was always the essence of the man: a creature that kills.

I swipe at him with the sword but he moves faster than I could have foreseen, leaping over the arc of the blade and bearing down on me. I step to one side but he still catches me with one hand, tearing a hole in my shirt – and in my shoulder – as he sails past. I try not to let it affect my aim as I bring the sword back and down, meaning to take off one of his legs when he hits the ground. We'll see how nimble he is after that!

But again Hagen is too quick for me, bouncing off the floor like a swimmer kicking off against a rock to give himself extra speed. The sword's blade connects with the floor and a ringing sound echoes around the hall. Hagen turns and steps in close. The smell of his breath is insufferable, burning my eyes. His hands move swiftly and he tears his nails across my chest, opening another wound that immediately begins to soak my shirt further with blood.

I lift a leg to kick him away and thus allow me room to use the sword but he pushes forward and we both fall to the floor, him on top. Like a dog Hagen goes for the neck, meaning to tear out my throat. He gives a sudden howl and rolls off me. It takes me a second to realise why. It would seem that Grost's foul garlic mixture works after all. I flip myself towards him, swinging the sword down on his back. There's not enough strength in the blow to do more than wound but the silver burns him and I'm relieved to hear him scream.

Hagen runs forward, moving on all fours and

charging towards the wall. I get to my feet, meaning to follow, but he jumps at the wall, bounces off it and sails over my head, getting in a solid blow to my cheek as he passes.

My eyes are full of blood and I'm forced to wipe them with my shirtsleeve while swinging the sword in front of me, hoping to keep Hagen at bay while I'm disadvantaged. I do more than defend myself – I actually get in a lucky blow, the sword cutting deep into the muscle of his right bicep. He screams again and backs away, holding his arm protectively before him.

I charge, not wanting to lose the advantage and he moves to run past me. But I get in another thrust, the silver blade hissing as it pierces his thigh.

Now! I have him!

'Hagen!' Lady Durward leaps on me and I watch as the creature limps through a shattered door on the opposite side of the hall.

Honestly, I trust the others to deal with one small detail . . .

Her arms reach around my neck and she brings her face close to mine, sucking in deeply. The effect is instant: a wave of tiredness engulfs me as she begins to drain the life from me.

I flip forward so that she rolls over my head and onto the ground, breaking the contact long enough for me to raise the sword in front of my face and point the mirror at her eyes.

She sighs, caught in her own gaze. I lift the sword and she gets to her feet. I turn in a circle and she follows, her stare never leaving the mirror. We are like dancers at a stately ball. I see the others are all under her spell – Grost, Gluckhaven and Carla – all staring into space as if they are daydreaming.

They are not cut out for this sort of work.

'You are a beautiful woman,' I say to Lady Durward, 'but your heart is cold. And you killed a very good friend of mine. A man who deserved better. I will send you to him so he can tell you himself how he feels about it.'

I pull the sword back and for a fraction of a second her eyes refocus, the spell of her own gaze broken. Then I swing the blade round and take her head from her body. That striking face turns slack and empty as the head spins away from me to land on the flagstones and roll into a corner. My friends, as one, have control of their minds returned to them. They all awake as if from a deep sleep.

The body crumples as the muscles in the legs lose strength and the whole carcass topples to the floor.

I look to see where the head has fallen. It stares life-lessly at the startled faces of Lady Durward's children.

To my surprise, Sara smiles slowly. 'Good,' she says, taking her brother's hand. 'Now do the same to that bastard of a father.'

Treat your children badly, I think, and sooner or later they will grow strong enough to make you regret it.

'I plan on doing just that,' I promise her.

'Sorry,' says Grost, 'she was just too fast.'

'Don't worry about it, my friend,' I say, patting him on the shoulder. 'All three of you are safe, and that's good enough for now.'

274

We move towards the open door, the darkness of a flight of steps beyond it. I hold my sword cautiously out in front of me.

'The cellars,' I say. 'It's down there. Bleeding and frightened, hiding in the dark.'

'Come on,' says Gluckhaven. 'Let's get after it while it's weak.'

I put a restraining hand on his arm. 'Weakness is relative, I will go alone. Leave me to do what I am good at, while you keep my friends safe up here.' I give him a sly smile. 'Or deal with it after it's killed me and comes back up. It all depends on how lucky I am!'

'Luck will have nothing to do with it,' says Grost. 'Go and kill that abomination.'

I nod, take a candle and step through the door, down into the darkness.

The cellars stink of death and I am aware that, more than ever, this is a nest that I am descending into. Hagen Durward does not remember his humanity.

There is the sound of scurrying in the darkness and I keep my sword raised. I wonder how effective Hagen's eyes are in the dark. I imagine, since he's chosen to live down here, that they're better than mine.

A gentle growl comes from some way away. He's leading me deeper.

I become aware of something beneath my feet and lower the candle to take a closer look. Bones. Wonder - ful. I have stepped into Hagen's larder.

Raising the candle to eye level again I come face to face with Kerro. Or what is left of him. He is hanging upside down, like a ripening pheasant. His colleagues are next to him, as is a young woman and an older man. These two are staff by the looks of them: they wear the uniforms of domestic service. I back away and immediately feel a rush of air as Hagen runs past, lashing out at my back as he passes. I swing the sword around in the hope of hitting him but he is long gone.

My back feels hot. Blood is running down to the waist of my britches. I cannot afford to play these games, otherwise I will be dead of blood loss and my corpse will be hanging up with the rest of them.

The problem is the candle. Without it I can't see but with it I'm an easy target, one that he can track right through the cellar. I snuff it out and poke it into my belt.

The darkness is now absolute and the cellars could be an infinite space. I am adrift in here, uprooted from the physical world. I close my eyes and hold the sword out in front of me. The darkness is only a disadvantage if I allow it to be so. I have other senses than my sight. I can hear Hagen as he scampers to and fro, like a fat rat here beneath the ground. I can hear him sniffing me out, that pustule-covered nose of his catching my scent . . . my *scent*.

I move forward, stepping as quietly as I can while I reach out for the hanging bodies.

My hand brushes a dead face. Kerro, I can tell from the beard. I turn and squeeze in between the hanging cadavers. The sword held with its blade up, touching my nose. I breathe out – slowly, quietly – and find my centre.

The others laugh at my meditation, I know. Because they do not understand it. They think it's about sitting still and having a short sleep. It is not. It is about becoming everything and nothing. About emptying yourself of every useless thought and placing yourself at the very centre of existence. About achieving a perfect state of calm. About becoming aware, *really* aware of the world and your place in it.

I can feel Hagen coming. I can hear the soles of his feet on the dusty bricks. I can hear his breathing, trying to sniff me out, trying to catch my scent above the sweet taint of his food store. I can even hear his heart, pounding in his chest. That engine of life, even for a vampire. The organ you rupture with your stake. Burn with the sun. Boil with Holy Water or *slice asunder with silver!*

I thrust the sword forward, yelling with triumph as I feel its point push against a resistance out there in the darkness. I step out from among the swinging carcasses, back into the real world, into the physical realm of the cellar beneath Durward Hall and the screaming, dying animal on the end of my sword.

I push forward even further and I feel the sword slide through the creature's back and embed itself in some - thing behind him. Hagen howls, pinned hopelessly.

I let go of the sword. I want to see.

I pull the candle from my belt and light it with the tinderbox in my pocket. In the warm orange light I see Hagen, pinned through the heart, the sword stuck fast in a wooden pillar. He convulses as the poisonous silver courses through him. His mouth is wide open, though it would seem he can no longer scream. His hands clutch at the air. His eyes are wide, catching the light from my candle and reflecting its hot fire like a pair of suns.

I watch him die. Slowly. And I consider it good.

Hagen slumps around the sword, and his flesh finally remembers the grave that he should have been in long ago. It rots from his corrupt bones and wastes away in pieces on the cold cellar floor. The last sound: his skeleton, breaking up and dropping, like hollow wind chimes, to the ground.

My job is done.

Fifty-Two

Carla Finds Her Road

When Kronos comes back up from the cellar he is not a pretty sight. And, given how good he normally looks, that tells you something.

'It is done,' he announces, in that stiff tone of his. And promptly walks through the drawing room and straight out of the house.

'It's a good job he's good at killing vampires,' I say, 'because he'd be adrift in life if he was forced to rely on his charm.'

Paul Durward is not a well man. He sits on the floor of the entrance hall, staring into space. 'Sorry, daddy,' he says as we walk over. 'I'm such a bad boy.'

'Go on,' says Sara. 'I'll look after him. Always have, always will.'

I look to Freddie, thinking that he may suggest some - thing. But he simply shakes his head and leads me outside.

'That's their mess,' he says once the cool of a late summer breeze has gone some way towards clearing the smell of death from our nostrils. 'Let them deal with it.'

And with that he starts to cry. I hold onto him and we

sit down on the front step while he lets out every last bit of sadness for the woman he loved. No, *loves*. Her death hasn't changed his feelings – only time will do that.

'Look.' Grost stands in front of us, shifting awkwardly and looking after Kronos who is climbing on his horse and riding away. 'I had better . . .'

'Come here first,' I say.

I kiss him and whisper into his ear: 'Never stop fighting the monsters you beautiful man.'

He looks at me and I realise that he may be about to cry as well. What is it with men these days?

'Go on!' I say. 'And look after him.'

'Thank you.' He runs after Kronos, climbs on his own horse and gallops away.

I doubt that I shall see either of them again.

'Sorry,' says Freddie, wiping at his face. 'So stupid . . .'

'Not at all,' I tell him. 'You've earned the right to shed every single tear.'

He sniffs and looks up at the stars. Sighs, rubs at his face. 'We did well,' he says eventually.

'Yes,' I agree. 'Very well. And now there's a choice: either you let go of the past and find your future or you become like those two.' I nod towards where the sound of horses can still be heard. 'Which is it to be?'

'What are you going to do?'

'Doesn't matter about me,' I tell him. 'I've got my road. It starts here and ends up who knows where. I'll find out when I get there.'

'It might be horrible,' he says, smiling slightly.

'Or it might be the best place you ever saw.'

'True.'

And one day we'll find out.